CHARTER ROAD

STING

of the

SEER

PublishAmerica
Baltimore

© 2005 by Charter Road.
All rights reserved. No part of this book may be reproduced, stored in a retrieval system or transmitted in any form or by any means without the prior written permission of the publishers, except by a reviewer who may quote brief passages in a review to be printed in a newspaper, magazine or journal.

First printing

At the specific preference of the author, PublishAmerica allowed this work to remain exactly as the author intended, verbatim, without editorial input.

ISBN: 1-4137-8580-8
PUBLISHED BY PUBLISHAMERICA, LLLP
www.publishamerica.com
Baltimore

Printed in the United States of America

This book is Christian fiction. Only the characters and references out of the *Holy Bible* are true. All other characters and references, with the exception of Charter Road, are fictitious, including places and establishments mentioned in real locations, and are not to be taken literally. Any resemblances are merely coincidental.

Cover art and design by *The MYSTIC* (*The More You See the Imagination of Christ*) *Graphics*, an affiliation with *Charter Road*.
Copyright © 2005 by *Charter Road*. All rights reserved.

Verses marked NKJV are taken from the *New King James Version*, copyright ©1979, 1980, 1982 by *Thomas Nelson, Inc*. Used by permission. All rights reserved.

Verses marked NIV are taken from the *HOLY BIBLE, NEW INTERNATIONAL VERSION* ®. Copyright © 1973, 1978, 1984 by International Bible Society. Used by permission of Zondervan Publishing House. All Rights reserved.

Special thanks to Kathy Perry, The Chance, and Chappy ♥ for all their help and encouraging words in the preparation of this book.

This book is dedicated to my Beloved, Lord and Savior, Jesus Christ. He is the Road that leads to eternal life.

1

Professor Jeremy Thompson trudged along the sandbanks of Egypt, pulling on the reigns of a very disagreeable one-humped camel named, Dunes. He stopped for a moment to take a drink from his canteen and groaned, "Ugh! My mouth is so blistered it feels like I have a fat lip."

Jeremy licked his cracked lips several times with his parched tongue and added, "I better put on more sunblock."

Rubbing protective ointment all over his face, he squinted at the blazing sun. Breathing shallowly, he wiped the sweat trickling down his neck with his shirt collar and groaned, "Whew! I feel like I'm melting out in this forsaken place. It's so hot out here, I can hardly breathe."

All at once, a huge swarm of flies buzzed past the Professor's head. He flinched and quickly brushed the right side of his cheek. Shading his baby blue eyes from the scorching sun, he stared intently at the passing flies. "Sand flies? What are they doing out here, Dunes? It looks like they're heading in the same direction we are. Boy, we're sure lucky those blood suckers didn't have time to stop for lunch. One bite from those devils could lead to *dum dum* fever. Now wouldn't that be a crying shame to die right before finding the greatest treasure in the world?"

The Professor frowned, thinking about the potential power insects have in transmitting diseases and then shook his head to dismiss the thought. "That's all right you cocky little buggers, it won't be long before you have to bow to me, provided I can ever figure out what that stupid riddle on the map means."

Jeremy's thoughts were suddenly interrupted when the buzzer sounded on his watch. He immediately shut off the alarm and checked the time. "Oh, it's four o'clock. I better take my medication."

He reached into his shirt pocket and pulled out a prescription bottle. Uncapping the lid, he put one of the psychotic pills into his mouth and then washed it down with water.

The instant the dry-mouthed camel eyed the water trickling into the Professor's mouth it started wailing for a drink.

"Are you thirsty, Dunes?"

"Raaaaaaaah, raaaaaaah!"

"Alright, let me grab another canister out of the pack. This one is empty. Here you go, boy. Fresh water from that stream we found a mile back."

As he poured the water into the animal's mouth it started choking. "What's wrong, Dunes? Did the water go down the wrong pipe? Heeheehee."

He patted the camel on the back until it finished choking and then said, "You want some more?"

The animal snarled at the canister and turned away, voicing loudly its discontent. "Naaaaaaah!"

"You sure weren't very thirsty. Come on, boy, take another drink. What's the matter with you? You act like there's something wrong with the water."

Jeremy sniffed the spout of the flask and shrugged. "It doesn't smell funny."

He poured some of the water into the palm of his right hand and then lapped it with his tongue. "It tastes like water. I don't know what your problem is, Dunes, unless the heat's getting to you."

Jeremy held the cupped water in his hand under the camel's mouth and said coaxingly, "Come on, Dunes, take a drink."

Again, the camel turned his head away in sour protest, groaning loudly, "Naaaaaaaah!"

The Professor scowled at the animal and said frustratingly, "What? There's nothing wrong with the water. I checked it."

"Raaaaaah, raaaaaah!"

"Okay, okay, I'll check it again. I don't know why you're acting so crazy, Dunes."

The Professor reluctantly poured more water into his hand and was astounded to see it turn into dust. He squealed in a shrill voice and tossed the canteen on the ground as if it were a poisonous snake. Then he spit the dust out of his mouth and slowly moved away from the canister, babbling distressingly, "What in the world is going on here? You mean that river wasn't real either? It was just another mirage like that phony kingdom I saw two days ago? Oh my goodness, I can't believe it. I filled all those flasks with dirt. That means we only have one good canteen left. Now don't get panicky, Dunes, we're going to find that guide and get the heck out of here."

Jeremy's dry eyes blinked rapidly from the intense heat as he slowly looked around the lonely desert. Then he reached into his shirt pocket and took out an ancient map written in hieroglyphics and a pair of bifocals. After affixing the spectacles to his face, he carefully examined the map against the compass in his hand. "I know I followed the right directions. I went four miles south, three miles west, and four miles northeast, just like it says."

Gaping at what appeared to be an endless sea of sand he mumbled questionably under his breath, "So where is this person? Maybe I better read the map again. 'Once you have gone four miles northeast, you will be sent a guide who will lead you the rest of the way.'"

"Yeah right, I've been wondering around in this sand trap for days and still no sign of a guide."

Jeremy was so stressed out he started throwing a little temper tantrum of kicking sand in the air, shouting contemptibly, "Uhhhhh! I'm never going to find that stupid charter! I'm just running around out here in circles wasting time!"

It didn't take long before the Professor physically wore himself out and sat down to rest. He put the compass in his shirt pocket and continued to question the validity of the map. Not being able to discern it, he hung his head down in despair and thought, *Maybe Charles' is right; maybe I am crazy for coming out here.*

Jeremy sighed heavily and then turned the map over. Refusing to give up, he made another desperate attempt to decipher the riddle of the pictorial characters on the back. While looking at different pictographs, consisting of an hourglass and three flies circling a cave hidden beneath the sands of Egypt, he pondered heavily on the clues, thinking aloud. "Cave time? Time cave? Time flies? I don't know."

He shook his head in frustration while putting the glasses back into his shirt pocket. "You know what, Dunes? I think I already have *dum dum* fever, because this dummy sure can't figure out the riddle. Hey, maybe I should give it to you, heeheehee."

Suddenly, without warning, a huge tornado appeared across the desert and whipped sand into his face. "Ow! Whoa, that wind almost sucked the map right out of my hand."

Jeremy quickly stuffed the chorography into his back pocket and then tightened his kaffiyeh to keep it from blowing away. Shouting to the top of his lungs in order to be heard above the galling wind, he queried, "Where did that twister come from, Dunes? There's no thunderstorm out here. It couldn't be a dust devil. I've never seen them get that big before. That thing must be over six hundred feet tall."

Skittish from hearing the devilish roar of the cyclone, the camel bleated, "Oooaaaah!"

Jeremy petted the side of the camel's cheek and said reassuringly, "Don't be scared, Dunes. It's okay, boy. I won't let anything happen to you."

Soon as the Professor steadied the camel, he took his protective goggles out of the pack and covered his eyes from the dusty wind. Staring with awe as he observed the huge whirlwind plowing its way across the desert, he said, "Wow! It's getting bigger. Look at the size of that thing. Man oh man, look at that baby go, whoopee."

Several moments passed before Jeremy noticed something peculiar about the cyclone. "Wait a minute…why is it changing shape like that? I've never seen a tornado do that before."

The inquisitive Professor peeked through his binoculars at the mystifying whirlwind and gasped in horror. "Get out of here, no way! Dunes, that's not a tornado. That's a giant vortex of sand flies, and those sand devils are coming right at us. We got to get out of here. Run! Come on, boy, run! Hurry! Faster!"

Jeremy ran through the desert like he was trying out for the Olympics until he stumbled and fell to the ground. As he watched the enormous cyclone of flies closing in on him from flat on his back, he thought his life was over. He scrunched his eyes tightly, not wanting to see the inevitable, until he felt something moving in the sand on the left side of him. With chills running down his spine, the Professor slowly turned his head to see what it was. Upon seeing an image of his face being formed out of the dust by the breath of the wind, he screamed with fright. "Aaaaaaaagh! What is that cursed thing?"

Without hesitation, Jeremy leaped to his feet and scampered away from the giant mold of sand being formed from the midriff up, and the huge vortex of flies that was now only a quarter of a mile away. He kept on running until he was completely exhausted and then stopped to catch his breath.

When he turned back around, he noticed the cyclone had moved to the other side of a huge dune. Right away, he grabbed the binoculars hanging around his neck and looked up at the devastating whirlwind of flies. He thought, *I don't believe it, that thing is sucking up sand like a giant vacuum cleaner. I wonder why?*

Jeremy pulled the binoculars away from his eyes momentarily to spit out more dust that had blown into his mouth. Then he peered back through the magnified lenses and suspiciously eyeballed the man of sand. Feeling intimidated by the appearance of the idol, he started stammering in a petrified squeak. "A dark Sa-Sandman, th-that loo-looks li-like me? How is that poss-possible?"

When he saw the Sandman grinning at him with admiration, his analytical mind compelled him to move a little closer so he could ask it a question, "Who-who are-are you?"

The Sandman promptly replied in a devilish wind that shook the desert sands, "The devil's breath!"

Jeremy's heart instantly flooded with terror as the ground trembled beneath him. All the hairs on his body stood up as he fearfully responded, "The de-de-devil's bre-breath?"

The ghostly Sandman nodded its head in agreement. Then it reached down and scooped up a huge pile of sand and blew it across the desert.

Jeremy's eyes looked like they were going to pop out of their sockets while watching the devil's breath turn all the desert dust into darkness. "Look at that, Dunes. All the light-colored sand has turned black."

The Professor started pacing back and forth nervously biting his fingernails. He still hadn't regained his composure from the last apparition he saw. "All right, Jeremy, get a grip. You're not going crazy. Just take another pill and all these phantoms will be gone."

Jeremy slowly inhaled a few deep breaths to put to rest the hysteria welling up inside him and then swallowed down another pill.

Just when the Professor thought his frazzled nerves were calming down, the Sandman opened its mouth wide and released a hellacious humming sound. "Yikes! Why is it making that horrendous noise, Dunes? It sounds like it's calling for something."

Soon as Jeremy figured out the Sandman was summoning the huge cyclone of flies, he took off running with his camel fast as he could. Feeling he was at a safe enough distance, he stopped and bent over, coughing and panting heavily.

Jeremy had barely got his wind back when he heard a multitude of high-pitch screeches that made his skin crawl. He quickly cupped his hands over his ears and squealed in disgust, "Ugh! That's the worst sound I've ever heard in my life. What's going on over there, Dunes?"

The Professor yanked off his dusty goggles and intuitively peeked through his binoculars to get a closer look. "I don't believe what I'm seeing. That hideous thing is sucking up that huge whirlwind of flies. Those poor devils—I never knew flies could make a noise like that. It sounds awful."

After the Sandman had gulped down the last fly, Jeremy noticed its belly was rapidly protruding. He bared his straight ivory teeth in disgust and said shakily, "Sick! Now the stupid thing looks nine months pregnant."

The idol of sand slowly turned its head towards the Professor and snickered at him like he was a doting fool.

"Good grief, Dunes! That thing's belly has gotten so big it looks like it's about ready to explode."

Jeremy had barely spit out the words when the Sandman's stomach suddenly burst open, disbursing millions of rambunctious sand flies into the air. Then, for no apparent reason, the idol turned back into dust. The swarm of flies that had ascended out of its belly headed back towards the huge dune and then vanished on the other side.

Jeremy was completely stunned by the rapid disappearance of the mystical Sandman. He rubbed his eyes several times thinking he was having another hallucination and then peered back through the binoculars. "That's the weirdest-looking thing I've ever seen in my life, Dunes. And lately, I've seen a lot of weird things."

The Professor waited for about twenty minutes before he felt it was safe to examine the area where the mysterious man of sand had emerged. When he returned to the spot, he knelt down and stared speechless at the huge pile of ebony sand. "Black sand? That's absurd. My eyes must be playing tricks on me again. There's no way that can happen, absolutely no way. It is virtually impossible for the sand to be turned into darkness unless its molecular structure had impurities....impurities?"

"You know what, Dunes? That Sandman formed out of dust reminds me of an article I recently read in a magazine while I was waiting to see the psychiatrist. It was a religious piece referenced from the Bible about Adam and Eve and the serpent in the garden. The write-up told how God formed man out of the dust of the ground. Then He breathed the breath of life into his nostrils, and he came to life. As long as Adam and Eve did not turn against the breath or Word of God, they wouldn't die."

"Anyway, the story went on to say how the original serpent, alias the devil, used his venomous breath to deceive Eve into disobeying God. Once he had poisoned her soul with his impure thoughts, her *"right"* thinking became paralyzed, and it wasn't long before she convinced her husband, Adam, to break the rules."

"Since the penalty for their sin was death, God removed His breath from their human bodies, and they slowly turned back into dust."

"What was the serpent's punishment? I'm glad you asked, Dunes. It said in the article that God cursed the tongue of the serpent for deceiving Eve and sentenced it to crawl on its belly and eat dust all the days of its life. According to the article, *"eating dust"* was supposed to represent a lowly condition in moral thinking, something disgusting you shook off the bottom of your feet, hahahaha. Some ancient piece of history, huh? Hahahaha! I think the commentary was kind of deep. I didn't fully understand it all anyway."

For a brief moment, Jeremy's thoughts were overwhelmed with sorrow as he thought aloud about the article. "Still, I can't deny the scientific fact that all humans die after losing their breath. That part of the story is true."

He scooped up a handful of sand that once formed the enchanted Sandman and slowly let it slip through his fingers. "I guess our lives are like the grains of sand in an hourglass, Dunes. We only possess a set amount of time before it runs out, and then we return back into a pile of dust."

The Professor pondered on the ghastly replica, still embedded in his mind, and started laughing insanely. "I can't believe it. That thing looked just like me and said it was the devil's breath. Either I'm still hallucinating, or I've gone stark raving mad."

The more Jeremy thought about being formed out of the devil's breath the angrier he got. He took in a lungful of air and then puffed the black dust out of his hands, snarling with indignation, "I'm not the devil's breath. I don't deceive people.

Talk about burying your head in the sand. I know for a fact there's no way possible any of that could happen. It must have been just another mirage. It had to be."

The Professor scratched his head in confusion and added, "But it seemed so real."

"You know what else puzzles me, Dunes? How was that cyclone of flies able to move at those incredible speeds? No ordinary insects can fly that fast. The breath of that foul wind they stirred up was incredible."

"Boy, if I'm dreaming all this up, I sure got quite an imagination. Maybe I should write a book about all my demented fantasies and call it, *Don't let this happen to you*, or *Have you snapped your twig?*"

The Professor chuckled heartily at his jesting and then looked back down at the huge pile of sand. He tried desperately to rid his mind of the ghostly image he saw but without much success. "That was so weird. I felt like I was talking to myself. What am I saying? I am talking to myself. Jeremy, you better get a grip. You're starting to lose it, buddy."

2

A gentle breeze swept through the dunes leaving artistic imprints as it kissed the grains of sand. Soon another wind would come and erase them all away.

Jeremy gaped at the sand being blown away by the wind with a sense of despair, thinking how easily his life could be forgotten. He wondered if there was any hope for him in the afterlife. He would soon find that out.

"Uh-oh, the wind is kicking up again! Dunes, where are you going? I need that tarp."

Jeremy quickly grabbed the huge canvas out of the pack on the camel's back and attached weights along the border to stop it from blowing away. "Okay, Dunes, quit complaining and get under there. Come on get under that tarp before this sand blisters me to death."

Sheltered under the protective covering, the two prisoners sat quietly listening to the howling of the wind.

Hours passed before the winds were finally replaced by a deadly silence. Jeremy broke the oppressive hush by whispering, "All right, boy, I think it's safe to come out now."

After removing the tarp, he tried pulling the grumbling camel to its feet. "Get up, Dunes! Come on, get up!"

When the rebellious animal failed to comply with his request, Jeremy slapped it hard on the butt, and the irritated camel tried to bite him on the leg as it stood to its feet.

"What's the matter, boy? Are you still mad at me for putting sand into your mouth? It's not my fault. I actually thought I was giving you a drink of water."

Jeremy pointed at the camel's face, chuckling loudly. "Honest, I didn't know that river back there was only a mirage." Dunes started complaining bitterly so the Professor shouted, "Oh cry me a river why don't you. I don't know what you're griping about. I'm the one who keeps making a complete fool out of himself by embracing things that aren't even there. Like that giant Sandman, and let's not forget that huge kingdom made out of fool's gold that slowly emerged out of the grains of sand, three different times in three different places."

"You know, now that I think about it, the dimensions of that kingdom were amazing. Its height was further than the eye could see, and its width seemed endless in either direction. I'm sure glad you couldn't be fooled, Dunes. You knew the kingdom wasn't real and walked right through it. It's a good thing too, or I'd probably still be standing there with gold dust in my eyes, wondering how to get to the other side."

"Waaaaaah, waaaaah!"

"Alright, alright, you don't have to keep rubbing it in. You had your laugh when I landed on my buttocks after attempting to sit on a throne that turned back into dust."

Jeremy brushed the sand off his derriere and said grouchily, "You'd think I would have gotten the message the kingdom wasn't real the second time it disappeared. But no, this idiot tried to sit on that lousy gold throne a third time and wound up with another butt full of sand—me and my sand castles. Either I've been out in the desert sun too long or my schizophrenic medication isn't working anymore."

The Professor folded up the canvas and said grimly, "After all I've been through, it's a wonder I'm still sane. Wait a minute...do sane people talk to their camels? Don't answer that."

While Jeremy was busy stuffing the tarp back into the pack, he heard a very faint buzzing sound. "What's that noise?"

Out of nowhere, a horde of sand flies zoomed past his head. "Oh no you don't, you're not getting away from me this time. I'm going to see what you little devils are up to—at a safe distance of course. Come on, Dunes."

Jeremy chased hard after the flies until he climbed to the top of a huge dune. Peering down at the gorge on the other side, he said astoundingly, "Oh my goodness, Dunes, what happened here? It looks like someone blasted a huge hole in the desert. Come on, boy, let's go down and check it out."

Pulling hard on the reigns of the winded camel, he scuttled down the lofty dune. Approaching the crater with extreme caution, he said, "Isn't it incredible, Dunes? I've never seen a hole that big before. If I didn't know better, I'd swear some invisible force had dug up a giant's grave. Do you suppose that oversized vacuum cleaner we saw earlier had anything to do with this?"

The Professor knelt down on the cushion of sand and carefully examined the bowl. "I wonder what's keeping the sides of the crater from caving in."

He gently touched the particles of dirt along the brim of the basin and added, "That's strange…all the grains of sand seem to be cemented together so they can't escape."

Jeremy cautiously stepped inside the crater and said surprisingly, "Now how can that be? It feels like rock under my feet."

Stomping his feet a little harder on top of the huge stones, he went on to say, "Hey, I think a couple of the boulders are loose. Come here, Dunes. I want to remove these blocks to see what's underneath. Come here, I need that rope. Oh quit your whining. I can't move these blocks by myself. They're too heavy."

The Professor tied the rope around Dunes' body and then wiped more sweat dripping down his neck with a handkerchief he took out of his back pocket. He struggled with the camel for about an hour before getting it to remove a couple of the boulders.

"Well what do you know, there really is a cave hidden down there. See, Dunes, I'm not crazy...I think."

The ecstatic Professor jumped up and down laughing excitedly. "Dunes, are we lucky or what? We didn't need that stupid guide. We found it all by ourselves by following those sand flies."

Peeking into the dark hole, the Professor groaned, "Ugh! Look at all the cobwebs and spiders. I sure hope this cave is not just another one of my hallucinations, or that would really put a damper on my trip."

"Hey, Dunes, did you hear that? There's that harmonious buzzing sound again. I heard it the first day we came out to the desert. It sounds like a bee is singing in my ear. If I didn't know better, I'd swear it was trying to warn me about something, hahahahaha. Isn't that ridiculous?"

Jeremy got down on bended knee and shouted into the cave. "Hello!"

An echo promptly replied, "Hello...Hello...Hello!"

"Dunes, I think we're going to need some light."

The Professor grabbed the flashlight out of his pack and then shined it into the mouth of the cave. Seeing a stairway of stone, he yelled, "Is anyone down there? Hello!"

Again, an echo shouted back, "Hello...Hello...Hello!"

Jeremy slowly crept down the long spiral staircase, brushing the cobwebs out of his way as he went along. After taking a few more steps, he stopped and shined the light up on the ceiling. "Wow! Look at the height of that ceiling. You'd think somebody had buried a dead god down here or something."

The Professor rubbed his beard in wonderment and then continued along the stairs. When he finally reached the bottom of the staircase, the light from his flashlight revealed an image engraved on the wall. He immediately moved closer to the slab of stone and squinted at the etching. "Hmm, that looks like a picture of an hourglass with only a few grains of sand left at the top."

He promptly put on his glasses and carefully examined the inscriptions. "Why aren't these depictions covered over with dirt?"

Taking a closer gander, he added, "Now isn't that interesting, they appear to be freshly written."

Jeremy took the chorography out of his back pocket and compared the drawings with the hieroglyphics on the wall. When he discovered the pictures carved in stone were exactly the same as those on the map, he raised an eyebrow and said, "I don't get it. What in the world is a time fly?"

He thought about it for a moment, but when nothing would come to mind, he shrugged his shoulders and walked away to examine another panel of stone. This time he saw an hourglass with black sand and carvings of bald Egyptian priests, shackled with chains around their wrists and ankles. Staring intently at the picture of the three priests bowing down to flies he said coldheartedly, "Stupid fools! You let the devil deceive you into worshipping a fly. I wonder what possessed you to do something so idiotic."

After amusing himself by laughing at the pictures on the wall, Jeremy suddenly realized the sunlight shining outside was slowly disappearing. He checked the time on his wristwatch and said, "Six o'clock? Where did all the time...fly?"

As the understanding finally sunk into his head, the Professor immediately diverted his attention to the hourglass and the flies etched on the wall. He spouted cheerfully, "Time flies!"

Snickering at the idol worshipping priests, he said, "Time flies when you're having fun, huh boys?"

Feeling extremely disappointed while looking down at the map, he complained ungraciously, "What kind of directions are these anyway? Time is running out. Running out for what? How do you expect me to find you with instructions like these?"

He gazed around the dark dusty room and bellowed, "Do you hear me, Baal-zebub? Where is the bible you promised me that will give me the faith to become like you? Answer me!"

Jeremy soon became discouraged when no one answered. He scrunched the map tightly in his hand and shouted, "I can't believe I came all the way out here on some wild goose chase. How could I be so stupid?"

Once more, the echo reiterated, "Stupid…Stupid…Stupid!"

The Professor hurled the chorography against the wall, screaming bitterly, "Aaaaaagh! All that time wasted for nothing. What an idiot! I should have listened to Charles when he told me not to come out here."

When he had finished feeling sorry for himself, he quickly changed his tone. "Oh well, hopefully I can find my way back here with a team of archeologists so the trip's not a total loss."

He sighed heavily and groaned, "I guess it's time to get out of here."

3

The disenchanted Professor headed toward the stairs until he saw two circular lights glowing on the wall. Shining the light in their direction, he saw a picture of three blind priests with their arms lifted up towards two golden suns. He laughed, "You blind fools. Everyone knows there's no such thing as two suns."

Desperately wanting to find logic to all this madness, he reached out and touched the circular image on the right with his index finger. Instantly, he felt a sharp sting and withdrew his hand. "Ouch! Oh that smarted."

Jeremy licked his scorched finger several times to soothe his throbbing pain and queried, "The picturesque of the sun is hot? Now how can that be when the rest of the wall is cold?"

He nervously tugged on the left side of his mustache while continuing to observe the two glowing suns. "I wonder what these two suns are supposed to represent anyway. Hmm, the one on the left has a deep depression in its belly, like something was taken out of it."

Thinking he was going to get burned again, the Professor squeezed his eyes tightly and then slowly put his unsteadied finger inside the crater of the sun. Feeling another sting, he shook his hand rapidly and barked, "Ow! That was icy cold!"

After blowing hard on his finger, he said touchily, "I don't get it. How come that sun is cold?"

Before he knew what hit him, a stream of electricity bolted out of the deflated circle and knocked him across the room. Overwhelmed with fear as he slammed into the wall, he raised his voice and said, "What the heck was that?"

The Professor cautiously stood to his feet and noticed the current had burned a huge hole in his shirt. He gently touched the singed area on his chest and cringed. "Ouch! Oh that stings. I don't believe it. That stupid sun tattooed a black ring on the center of my chest."

While preoccupied with examining the mark on his body, a stone panel suddenly opened in the ground directly below the two suns and startled him. Peering wary-eyed across the room at the underground trap, he wondered if it was safe to investigate. After a few moments of listening to the lamenting wind outside, his confidence and adventurous spirit returned, and he slowly approached the opening.

Soon as Jeremy saw the compartment filled with sand, he laid the flashlight down and dropped to his knees to tunnel through the dirt. He dug frantically for about an hour until he uncovered a small wooden treasure chest overlaid in gold. Pulling the box from the sand, he shouted in a voice of great expectation, "Yes! This has got to be it. The charter must be in here."

The giddy Professor kissed the side of the container and then danced merrily around the room, chuckling fanatically. Then he picked up the flashlight and looked around for a stone to break the padlock. After searching the vicinity without success, he took the chest and smashed it against the wall several times until the rusty lock fell off.

Opening the lid, he shined the light into the box and saw two small modern-day books and a gem bag, made out of the finest silk money could buy. Jeremy eagerly picked up the crimson-colored bag, thinking there were precious stones inside. Shaking the pouch next to his right ear, he said disappointedly, "It doesn't sound like there's anything in it."

The Professor slowly opened the bag and was surprised to see a tiny papyrus scroll hidden inside. He bellyached uninterestingly, "Oh no, it can't be, not another stupid message."

Glancing back into the empty bag, he griped in a snit, "That's it, just a stupid note? Where are the gems? If this is somebody's idea of a sick joke it's not very funny."

Jeremy angrily threw the bag on the ground and stomped on it. Afterward, he reached into the box and picked up the gray-covered book titled, *Baal-zebub, Lord of the Flies,* which had three black rings intertwined on the front cover. Relieved he found what he came after he brushed the dust off the cover and said happily, "I knew I'd find you."

Peeking back into the box, he eyed the etching of three united gold rings on the burgundy cover of the *Holy Bible*. He frowned and said in a voice of irritation, "What's this book doing in here? I'm not interested in this."

Jeremy stared bafflingly at the logos on both books, wondering what the three interconnected rings meant; especially since he now had a black ring branded on his chest. "I know the ring signifies a guarantee of a merger between entities, and it also symbolizes something that has no beginning and no end. But why three rings?"

The Professor thought it over very carefully, but when he couldn't figure it out, he decided not to question it anymore. He nervously scratched the left side of his cheek with the unholy bible and then put it back into the box. After setting the chest on the ground, he unrolled the miniature scroll and started translating the Hebrew inscriptions aloud. "Set before you is life or death. Choose your treasure wisely that you may live."

Skeptical, Jeremy laughed, "You mean I have a choice. Give me a break."

When he had finished snickering childishly, he continued reading the note aloud. "One son will destroy you so choose your words wisely that you may live."

He anxiously stroked his beard while mumbling under his breath, "Destroy you? I hope you're kidding."

Sensing something wasn't quite right, he gazed around the cave thinking, *Could all this be surrealistic?*

Then he remembered a conversation he once had with his friend, Charles.

"No, Charles. For the last time, stop preaching to me about your God."

"Jeremy, don't you get it? Time is running out. Everyone who denies the truth about Jesus will remain forever in an unreal world of deception. Please, ask Jesus into your heart before it's too late."

The Professor glanced back at the hourglass, still considering the things Charles had said. He nervously twisted the edge of his mustache and then turned the parchment over. After thinking about what the symbolism meant, he finished reading the message aloud. "The sun rules the day, and the moon rules the night."

Jeremy remarked sarcastically, "Now what is that, some sort of allegorical poetry? Why can't you speak in plain English for goodness sake?"

Now totally confused, he glanced back at the etching of the two suns. "If the brightness of the sun is supposed to represent Jesus, the Son of God, then everything revolves around the Son like Charles said. I wonder if he's right. Does the sun epitomize the brilliance of the almighty God? If that's true the other sun has got to be a fake."

Jeremy shook his head in frustration at this puzzlement and tossed the scroll on the ground. Picking up the chest, he stared apprehensively at the two books in the box. "I don't want to make the wrong choice. Which book contains the truth? Which one is really the voice of God?"

Flipping through the pages of the burgundy-covered book, Jeremy remembered Charles telling him that the *Holy Bible* contained the thoughts of Jesus. Closing the book, he thought uncertainly, *Could Jesus actually be the true Son, the bright shining voice of the almighty God?*

Fixing his eyes back on the wall, his jaw tinged when he noticed the sun on the left was losing its light. "It's turning into darkness—just like a lunar eclipse."

He boldly declared in self-assurance, "It was a fake. I was right. One of them is masquerading as the Son of God. Because everyone knows the heart of the moon has no true light of its own."

Glancing down at the two books in the box, he muttered under his breath, "But which one?"

Jeremy was determined to figure out the riddle so he mulled it over and over in his mind. *The sun rules the day, and the moon rules the night. The sun rules the day, and the moon rules the night.*

All of a sudden, He excitedly articulated, "Hold on, the sun is coming up. I think I just figured it out. They're different as night and day. I remember Charles telling me one time that day and night were used in ancient times as metaphors for good and evil. If that's true, I better be real careful which words I choose, like the note said."

Reaching out to grab the *Holy Bible*, he suddenly felt overwhelmed with doubt. Pulling his hand back, he shook his head and skeptically avowed, "No! I'm not going to get burned again. Nobody in his right mind would believe that this Jesus, who's supposed to be the Son of God of all people, would willingly die on a cross like Charles said. Why would Jesus allow

Himself to be crucified to pay the price for a bunch of sinners like me? Why would He do that? Why would He pay the ransom with His life's blood?"

Jeremy stared open mouthed at the Bible and thought restlessly, *But what if the story's true? What if Jesus did in fact prove He was the Son of God by rising from the dead and returning to heaven like Charles said? Then all I have to do is believe Jesus paid for my sins by asking Him into my heart, and God will give me eternal life.*

The Professor's heart was so filled with anxiety about making the wrong choice that he started pacing back and forth biting his lip. "I don't know, I just don't know. If I don't put my faith in Jesus to save me from sin, it could cost me eternity and a trip to hell."

Thinking it over very carefully, he finally blurted out, "No! It can't be. This is a trick. These thoughts are too good to be true. Nobody gets anything for free in life. There's always a catch."

Feeling sure of himself, he grabbed the gray-covered book out of the box and arrogantly affirmed, "I'll take the treasure I came after. I believe this one is the voice of God."

Jeremy had barely finished speaking when sand started falling on top of his head from a crack in the ceiling. He coughed several times from inhaling the dust and quickly moved out of the way.

While removing the dusty kaffiyeh from his head, a strong wind kicked up out of nowhere and blew the *Holy Bible* open. Jeremy shined the light on the manuscript, and the words, "Escape from Idolatry," leaped at him from off the page. Instantly he became paranoid and threw the treasure box containing the *Holy Bible* on the ground.

Swallowing hard, the Professor slowly backed away from the treasure chest. He kept a suspicious eye on the box for several moments until his inquisitive nature compelled him to open the unholy bible in his hand. After thumbing his way through the dusty pages of the book, he soon became disillusioned. "No. It can't be. The pages are all blank."

He shook the book vigorously, hoping to find a message he had overlooked. But when nothing but sand poured out, he became enraged and bellowed, "Where is the knowledge you promised me? Baal-zebub, you liar!"

The echo promptly mocked him back, "Liar…Liar…Liar!"

Jeremy went through the motions of showing the darkness the empty pages in the book while bitterly pointing out, "How can I become like you if I can't see you? Some voice of god you are; you're nothing but an empty belly if you can't keep your word."

Walking back towards the picture of the lunar eclipse, he slammed the book closed and glared at the cover. He chortled, "Lord of the flies, ha. How can you be lord of anything when you're too stupid to express yourself?"

The highly agitated Professor threw the empty manuscript against the wall and picked up the treasure box, noticing the *Holy Bible* was gone. After searching frantically for the missing book, he finally gave up. Thoroughly confused, he placed his right hand on his forehead and said, "I don't get it. Where did you go? I wanted you to talk to me."

Suddenly, from behind him came the earsplitting sound of angry buzzing. Dropping the box, he covered his ears and slowly turned around, shouting, "Who's there?"

Once more, he heard an echo mocking him, "Who's there…Who's there…Who's there?"

As the drumming got louder, Jeremy could hardly hear himself think anymore. He finally cried out, "Stop it! I can't stand it anymore. Stop it!"

The aggressive humming abruptly ended, and the Professor let out a huge sigh of relief as he uncovered his ears.

Shining the light around the room to see if he was still alone, he noticed the pictures on the wall had changed. The sun on the right had vanished, and the priests were lying on the ground dead. Horrified, he shook his head and slowly backed away. "No way, this is getting too weird. I'm getting out of this hellhole!"

4

The panic-stricken Professor looked like he'd just seen a ghost as he dashed up the stairs. He was just about to reach the top of the steps when he heard a high-pitch noise. Feeling curious, he cautiously tiptoed back down the stairs, inching his way over to the wall. Laying his ear to the stone, he shouted, "Is anybody in there?"

Pushing hard against the slab of stone, he hollered louder, "Can you hear me?"

Just then the light inside his flashlight began to dim. He hit the flashlight against his hand several times, whimpering upsettingly, "I just put new batteries in. Come on, work you stupid thing!"

Unfortunately, his efforts were futile and the light faded out. The Professor sighed in discontent, "Great, now I'm really in the dark."

After groping about in the darkness for several minutes trying to find his way back to the stairs, he heard noisy buzzing sounds as if there were a huge swarm of angry flies in the room. Thinking they were sand flies, he cried out timidly, "I said who's there?"

Right away, the room filled with an eerie glow. The Professor's eyes quickly adjusted to see thousands of fireflies emitting a cold black light while flying directly in front of him. "Fireflies, what are they doing in here?"

Jeremy took a moment to coax one of the fireflies on to his hand. "Come here beetle. Come on little fellow. I want to check you out."

After carefully examining the insect, the Professor stroked his beard and said with a false sense of superiority, "This can't be. It is scientifically impossible for your abdominal glands to produce a black light. Take my word for it little bug, this is years of science talking. You must be just another figment of my imagination."

He chuckled as the insect flew away. "Boy, for an apparition, you sure feel real."

Just when Jeremy thought he couldn't be more baffled by the mystical bugs, the fireflies started moving in formation like a well-drilled army to spell out words in all capital letters.

I AM YOUR GUIDE.

The Professor stared catatonically at the insects spelling the enchanted words, mumbling confoundedly under his breath, "The fireflies are using their bodies to spell words? I don't believe it."

Jeremy was so overwhelmed by the paranormal writings that he soon became completely spell-bound. Before he knew it, he was conversing with the little bugs. He snickered arrogantly, "My guide? So tell me guide, who are you?"

SIMPLETON, I AM BAAL-ZEBUB, LORD OF THE FLIES, WHO DO YOU THINK?

"I heard you were only a mythical god."

THEN WHY ARE YOU HERE?

Insulted by the dark lord's question, the Professor replied with unpleasant farce, "Why am I here? What do I got to do, spell it out for you, or wouldn't a real god know the answer to that question?"

Jeremy chuckled mischievously at his uncanny wit and said, "Touché."

QUIT WASTING MY TIME, HUMAN. YOU ARE HERE BECAUSE YOU BELIEVE WHAT YOU READ ABOUT ME.

IF YOU WANT TO BECOME LIKE ME, I CAN MAKE THAT HAPPEN.

Astounded by Baal-zebub's intellect, the Professor confidently declared in an awing tone, "You must be the real son of god, or how could you know that?"

All of a sudden, the wall slowly opened to reveal a room filled with black light.

COME INTO THE LIGHT.

Jeremy was completely captivated by the mystical god and felt led to obey its command. Only the moment he stepped into the room, the artificial light disappeared. Feeling put upon, he shouted in dry humor, "Another dark room? Let me guess, you didn't pay your electricity bill, right?"

When no one answered, Jeremy began to get impatient. He looked around the dark eerie room and bellowed in a disrespectful tone. "Oh Mister Baal-ze...*bub,* or whatever your name is. Do you hear me? Hello! Hey, *bub,* you promised to give me knowledge so I could become a god like you."

Suddenly, Jeremy smelt a horrible odor in the room and started coughing and gagging. "Pew, what's that horrible stink? It smells like something dead in here."

Feeling queasier as the stench grew stronger he quickly grabbed the handkerchief out of his back pocket and covered his nose and mouth. "Ugh! I got to see what's causing that awful smell."

Jeremy smacked the flashlight against the palm of his hand, trying hard as he could to get it to work, until he heard the continuous humming sound of a horde of angry bees. He shouted frightfully, "Who's there?"

Growing more restless as the droning increased, he hit the flashlight again. "Come on, turn on you stupid thing! I got to see what's going on in here."

Finally, after giving the flashlight a couple more whacks, the light came back on, exposing hundreds of thousands of bee flies spelling out words on the wall: YOUR THOUGHTS. Repugnance rapidly enveloped the Professor's mind as he heard the words buzzing inside his head. He choked and coughed on the unpleasant smell in the room and then distastefully blurted out, "My thoughts?"

Jeremy was so offended by the blunt innuendo that he lost his grip on the flashlight, and it broke hitting the ground. Feeling testy from standing in the dark, he griped, "Oh great! Now what am I going to do?"

Suddenly, to his surprise, the room flooded with black light. When the Professor saw the insects glowing under the synthetic light, he was completely overwhelmed by this supernatural phenomenon. He studied them closely with his scientific mind as the flies continued to form themselves into words. Shaking his head in uncertainty, he queried, "Fluorescent spelling bees? Charles is never going to believe this."

WE ARE ATTRACTED TO YOUR HEART. IT WILL MAKE A SUITABLE MEDIUM.

Jeremy snapped sharply, "What are you talking about? It smells like dung in here and...oh no...flies are attracted to dung."

The Professor quickly covered his nose with the handkerchief and started running. Only the moment he did, a huge dragonfly shackled in chains appeared directly in front of him. The creature had searing red compound eyes and wore a huge gold crown etched with pictures of ancient dragons.

Jeremy felt his lungs being paralyzed with fear as he stared face-to-face with the enormous beast. His feeble legs started shaking uncontrollably, and his lips began to quiver. Straight away, he shrunk back and squealed in a high-pitch stutter, "Tha-that's the big-biggest Aus-Aus-Australian Em-Emerald Dra-Dragonfly I've ever see-seen."

The beast scowled at Jeremy, snorting like an angry bull.

"Ple-please, I'm not-not a fl-fly so do-don't ea-eat me."

The Professor had to admit, things looked pretty grim as he eyed the razor-sharp jagged teeth sticking out of the creature's mouth. He shuddered at the thought of being eaten alive by this monstrosity and wondered how he was going to get away.

After an hour of standing frozen in one spot while being closely inspected by the beast, Jeremy's legs began to buckle. He slowly backed away from the drooling monster, nervously cracking his knuckles. Then he crawled into the far corner of the room and sat down, trying hard to keep awake.

When the Professor couldn't stand the quiet in the room anymore, he started jabbering stupidly, "Is this what you really look like Mister Baal-zebub? My goodness, you're the most beautiful specimen of a dragonfly I have ever seen. If you don't mind me saying so, I think I'm pretty impressive too, for a human being that is. I just snap my fingers and the ladies come running. Heeheehee."

The Dragonfly smirked at the male egomaniac and then belly laughed at him as if he were some sort of comic.

"Oh good, you're laughing. If you're laughing, then you're not thinking about devouring me, I think. The only problem is I don't know what I'm going to do for an encore."

5

Jeremy took the binoculars off his neck and laid them on the ground. Rubbing the tender spots on his neck left by the straps, he leaned back against the wall. While continuing to study the Dragonfly's bizarre behavior, he noticed the creature wasn't casting a shadow. He nervously stroked the sides of his mustache, questioning in the back of his mind, *Is that thing real?*

Earnestly desiring the truth, the Professors' eyes were suddenly opened to see phantom bugs. Taken aback by what he saw, he gasped, "The Dragonfly and the other insects are only apparitions? Are my eyes playing tricks on me again?"

He quickly removed his glasses to wipe the dust off the lenses and then put them back on his face. "I still see ghosts, false images appearing to be real."

Concerned about his own image, he gradually stood to his feet and checked his shadow on the wall. The moment he did, he saw his silhouette change into the shadow of a tiny bee fly. Instantly, paranoia coursed through his veins, and he started screaming hysterically in operatic montages.

The Dragonfly sneered at the noisy human and then whistled an order to the ghostly bee flies. Without hesitation, the buzzing insects started forming themselves into words: *WHAT'S THE MATTER, HUMAN? ARE YOU AFRAID OF YOUR OWN SHADOW?*

The Professor clenched his jaw to stop his teeth from chattering and then replied in a pitiful squeaky voice, "Ye-ye-yes."

GOOD. THAT MEANS YOU SEE ME AS A GIANT AND YOURSELF AS A PATHETIC LITTLE INSECT THAT I CAN EASILY SQUASH.

The beast's murderous threats intensified Jeremy's uneasiness, causing him to stammer breathlessly. "I do-don't wa-want to be squa-squashed; I got-got to ge-get out of here-here."

Keeping an eye out, the Professor anxiously looked around for a way of escape. Seeing the perfect opportunity, he darted towards the exit. However, before he could reach the edge of the stairs, the creature stirred a strong wind by flapping its giant wings and thumped him to the ground.

When the Dragonfly noticed the human was too frightened to get up, it came closer to study him. As the huge beast peered curiously into Jeremy's eyes the adrenaline surged through his body. His heart was beating so fast he thought it was going to explode out of his chest. He tried to choke back the fear, but the anxiety could be easily heard in his voice. "Please, uh, do-don't uh, e-eat me-me."

The creature grinned amusingly at the encumbered human, watching him stumble over his words. "Uh, uh, who-who-who are you?"

Jeremy inhaled several deep breaths to calm his nerves while the buzzing bee flies quickly spelled the word: BEELZEBUB.

The Professor gulped another deep breath and thought, *Beelzebub? Isn't that a Greek word for "god of dung?"*

I AM YOUR LORD.

After cringing from the stench of the Dragonfly's breath, Jeremy belittled the beast by thinking, *My lord? I know I've been told I'm full of poop before, but this is ridiculous.*

SEER, I HAVE CHOSEN YOU TO SPEAK FOR ME.

The Professor's heart instantly filled with hate upon reading the egotistical words and found it much easier to speak. "Not-not me, bub; I'm not crazy about the smell."
SO WHY SPEAK THE WAY YOU DO?
"I don't know. Maybe I'm just a dummy," he snapped sarcastically.
Suddenly, the fireflies reappeared in the room as fluorescent ghosts and swiftly formed their luminous bodies into words: YOUR WORDS TURN ME ON.
Flabbergasted by what he read, Jeremy stood to his feet and gasped, "What?"
When the lightning bugs had finished spelling the words, they started hovering around the Professor's head. Annoyed by the little pests, he swatted at them, shouting belligerently, "Get away from me! What's with you stupid bugs? You act like you're in heat."
The Dragonfly whistled its influential power over the fireflies, and they stopped harassing Jeremy and started spelling out words: WOULDN'T A REAL PROFESSOR OF ENTOMOLOGY KNOW THE ANSWER TO THAT QUESTION?
Jeremy turned up his nose at the beast's cheeky remark and said, "Cute."
Then he glanced towards the stairs, plotting a way of escape. After a brief moment of yawning and stretching, he mocked the creature again by saying, "You know what? I suddenly feel all pooped out. So I guess you don't need me anymore."
He snickered about his uncanny wit until a roll of toilet paper appeared in his right hand. He said scornfully, "Why you little poop."
Baal-zebub's laughter flooded the cave.
"Har-har-har-har, you think you're so funny."

Grumbling under his breath, Jeremy threw the roll of toilet paper at the swarm of fireflies and cynically declared, "I hate bugs! I used to love the little creatures, but now I hate them." The Dragonfly whistled again and the buzzing bee flies rapidly spelled the words: BEELZEBUB and BAAL-ZEBUB.

Jeremy snickered under his breath, "Beelzebub and Baal-zebub; some dynamic duo, lords of flies and poop."

He shook his head in disgust and subsequently stared back at the names on the wall. Mumbling quietly to himself, he said, "Somehow, I think the two are connected to each other, but how? I wonder if one lord is using the other the way the fly uses the dung. Wait a minute, isn't Beelzebub also an alias for...."

Before he had time to think another thought, the bee flies circled him and started buzzing hostilely. Unsettled by their aggressive tone, Jeremy slowly took two steps backwards and said timidly, "Uh-oh, I think it's time to fly. Now boys, don't get upset. I know you still want to talk, so I'll tell you what, I'll give you a ring or a buzz sometime."

He snickered under his breath and added, "Yeah right, in about a hundred years."

All at once, Jeremy dashed towards the stairs. But he didn't get very far before the angry horde of bee flies attacked him. Waving his arms frantically in a desperate attempt to fight off the stinging flies, he screamed hysterically, "Aaaaaaaagh, aaaaaaagh! Get off me! Aaaaaaaaaagh!"

It was quite evident Jeremy was fighting a losing battle. Covered with flies from head to toe, he slowly dropped to his knees, still screaming uncontrollably. Collapsing to the ground, his bifocals fell off his face and busted.

Again, the Dragonfly whistled commandingly, and the teed off bee flies hastily retreated to spell out the words: SPEAK FOR ME.

The Professor squinted at the message and responded in a frail, raspy voice. "I can't see what you're spelling. You broke my glasses."

Jeremy sneered at the beast and then started removing stingers out of his swollen face the size of thorns. "Ow! Ow! Ouch! Ooooh, that hurts. Ow! Ouch! Oh, that one smarted." Tears flowed down his cheeks as he whimpered miserably, "This can't be happening. Bee flies don't have stingers. Besides, you're just ghosts. You can't inflict pain."

The bee flies quickly spelled the words: THE MOMENT YOU BELIEVED US TO BE REAL WE CAME INTO YOUR REALM. YOUR FAITH ENABLES US TO STAY.

Suddenly, he jumped when the bifocals appeared in his hand. After careful inspection, he said in a voice of surprise, "They're not broken. How did you do that?"

Putting on the glasses, he looked over at the message on the wall and started reading it aloud. "The moment you believed us to be real we came into your realm. Your faith enables us to stay."

He thought, *I wonder if that's why his image faded when I started doubting him. If that's true, how do I get more faith to send Baal-zebub back into the dead realm he came out of?*

HUMAN, WHY DO YOU HAVE THAT STRANGE LOOK ON YOUR FACE?

The Professor replied sarcastically, "I've had a lot of strange looks since I met you. Which one in particular are you referring to, hysteria, stupidity, depression, rage, terror, nausea, or is it horror? Heeheehee."

While Jeremy was busy wiping the blood off his face with his handkerchief, a vanity mirror appeared directly in front of him. After flinching fearfully from the sudden manifestation of the mirror, he peered curiously into the glass. To his surprise, he saw the reflection of a dummy staring back at him. "What have you done to me? I'm a…I'm a…dummy!"

Before he could utter another sound, the reflection of thousands of ghostly fireflies became visible in the mirror, spelling out the words: DO YOU SEE YOURSELF AS A DUMMY, HUMAN?

Staring fixedly at their mirrored image, he angrily snapped, "Yes!"

The fireflies immediately spelled out the words: GOOD. THEN I'LL BE YOUR VENTRILOQUIST.

The Professor had barely finished reading Baal-zebub's arrogant reply when a devilish laughter filled the room and taunted his anguished soul.

Jeremy sarcastically reiterated, "Ha-ha-ha-ha."

Shortly afterward, the mirror and the image of the fireflies slowly faded away.

Jeremy checked his body over very thoroughly and noticed it was back to normal. Rubbing his eyes several times, he decided to check his skin again to make absolutely sure he was seeing correctly. When everything looked okay, he heaved a huge sigh of relief. "I'm not a dummy, and my wounds are gone. They were just figments of my imagination."

Jeremy took the prescription bottle out of his shirt pocket and threw it against the wall. "When I get back home, I need to have my doctor write me a new prescription. I don't think my schizophrenia medication is agreeing with me."

The Professor stared wide-eyed at the phantom insects for several moments and then whispered under his breath, "Wait a minute…fireflies and bee flies are both mimickers, creatures that deliberately deceive other living things."

He slowly peered around the room and went on to say, "This place has got to be some sort of deceptive realm."

Before Jeremy had time to finish pondering his thoughts on the estranged underworld, the huge Dragonfly opened its mouth wide and roared like a dragon. The haunting sound chilled the Professor's bones, frightening him out of his wits. Keeping his worried eyes glued on the beast hovering overhead, he thought, *Why do you have that stupid smirk on your face? What are you up to?*

Without warning, the ravenous beast opened its mouth wide and started sucking the life out of the flies in the cave. Not being able to withstand the powerful suction of the Dragonfly's breath, the frightened, screeching little bugs could not get away.

Jeremy was highly overwrought watching the merciless creature devour the last few flies into its rapidly protruding stomach. He whimpered cowardly, "You just ate all your little buddies. Some friend you are. Now who are you going to play with?"

The Dragonfly completely ignored the Professor's comical remarks and started sniffing him.

"I sure hope you're not still hungry," whined Jeremy.

Then he slid along the ground on his buttocks trying to get further away from the creature. "How could I be so stupid? I can't believe I picked evil. Charles always said I made bad choices in life, but this one's a doozie."

When the Dragonfly followed after him, Jeremy grumbled loudly, "I wish you would quit breathing down my neck!"

The Beast roared again at the irritated human. Then it took in a long deep breath and spewed fire out of its mouth. Soon as the Professor saw the flames coming towards him, he shut his eyes tightly, screaming in a panic, "Aaaaaaaaagh!"

Trembling at the thought of being turned into dust by cremation, he chanted over and over again, "I'm dead, I'm dead, I'm dead!"

Realizing he hadn't died in the blaze, he slowly opened one eyelid at a time and noticed the fire was gone. He let out a huge sigh of relief and then thought about the multitude of demonic voices he had heard inside the flames. The more he thought about it the sicker he felt.

"That was the most horrible ordeal I have ever experienced in my life. It was awful. The beast's thoughts burn against everything that is good. It absolutely has no mercy. I don't know why anyone in their right mind would want to speak for that thing. Goodness, I don't think I'm ever going to tell anyone to go to hell again."

THE FIRE DIDN'T HURT YOU BECAUSE YOU WORSHIP ME.

Jeremy responded in a distasteful whisper so the beast couldn't hear him. "Worship you? You got to be kidding me. Why in the world would anyone want to worship you unless they were deceived into doing it? I'm not going to make the same mistake those stupid priests made. I'm not going to worship something that has the brain mentality of a fly."

The Professor looked back at the pictures of the priests and said accusingly, "You chained those priests to your idolatrous thoughts. Your cold black heart made them prisoners of hell."

HOW DID YOU KNOW ABOUT THAT?

Staring hatefully at the beast, he answered pompously, "What do you mean how did I know about that? It's clear as the writings on the wall, and you call me a dummy."

WHAT WRITINGS?

"The pictures on the wall behind me," Jeremy barked impatiently.

Turning around, he was stunned to see the wall covered over with cobwebs and dirt. He slapped his hand over his mouth and gasped, "Where did they go?"

After roaming his eyes around the room, he scratched his head in bewilderment and added, "And what happened to the scroll and the treasure box?"

DID YOU HEAR ME, HUMAN? WHAT PICTURES?

Sick of all the optical illusions, Jeremy rubbed his temples in aggravation and shouted, "I heard you, never mind! Obviously it was nothing but another delusion like everything else I've seen."

The Professor crawled back into his corner and sat quietly, mulling over the creature's behavior. *Why are you in chains? And why do you believe you're a dragon? Are you bewitched?*

Jeremy picked up the gray-covered book off the ground, trying hard to think of the creature's alter ego. Several moments passed before he figured it out. "Oh no, now I remember. You think you're a dragon because Beelzebub is alias for...."

Panic swiftly struck at the heart of the Professor, and he started screaming in a voice of desperation. "Aaaaaaaaaagh! Some-some-somebody, help-help me, please!

The Professor immediately sprung to his feet and ran so fast he tripped climbing the stairs. Just as he was about to reach the top step, the ghostly Dragonfly grabbed the hysterical Professor and flew out of the cave.

Spotting his camel still waiting for him down below, Jeremy immediately shouted a verbal command the animal's master had given him in case he ran into any trouble. "Dunes, Meshach!"

Right away, the camel eagerly headed homebound, back to the safety of its small shack.

"When you get back to the hut, call 911. Tell them I got carried away by another hallucination. Aaaaaaaaaaaaagh!"

The Professor's terrifying screams gradually faded into the distance as the Dragonfly hauled him away into the night.

6

Professor Charles Chapman, a very distinguished-looking gentleman, stood before a classroom teaching Entomology to thirty tentative students at a reputable university in New Orleans. He paused briefly from his lecture on the fly to take a penlight out of his suit pocket and then flipped a control switch on the wall. Instantly, a retractable screen lowered from the ceiling showing a diagram of the different developmental stages of a fly.

After aiming the pen's red-colored beam at one of the pictures on the screen, he continued with his lesson. "Flies lay their eggs in a medium such as decaying animal flesh or dung. They go through a complete metamorphosis…egg, larva or worms, pupa, adult."

Charles adjusted his tie and said, "Now, are there any questions?"

One of the female students in the front row raised her hand.

Charles recognized her by saying, "Yes, Pam."

"Why do they put their eggs in dung?" she queried in her Louisiana accent.

"Because heat in dung acts as an incubator for the eggs. Are there any more questions on the material we've covered so far?"

Charles' eyes roved around the classroom to see if anyone else had raised his or her hand. Looking towards the back row, he spotted one of his female students reading a *Holy Bible*. Annoyed by her disinterest in the class lesson, he called out to her in a stern tone, "Destiny."

When she didn't acknowledge him, he cleared his throat and raised his voice, "Miss Vienna!"

Destiny slowly looked up at her teacher, hoping she wasn't in trouble.

"Is there something more interesting than my lecture on the fly?"

"Yes sir," she politely replied.

When the class laughed at her response, Charles crossed his arms in a huff and said pridefully, "Then maybe you'd like to share it with the whole class."

"Sure. I'd love to."

Charles stared annoyingly at the Australian beauty as she eagerly stood to her feet. Reading out of the *Holy Bible*, she quoted a passage of scripture with great zeal. "For I know the thoughts that I think towards you, says the Lord, thoughts of peace and not of evil, to give you a future and a hope." (Jeremiah 29:11 NKJV)

Charles brushed his naturally curly bangs to one side and then abruptly interrupted her. "That's very beautiful, Destiny. But in the future, if you want to read literature in this class, I suggest you stick to the textbook."

She respectfully answered back, "Yes sir."

The bell rang, and the students quickly jumped to their feet.

Charles shouted to be heard above the bustle in the room. "Don't forget, there will be a test on this material next Tuesday!"

One of the male students grumbled to his girlfriend on the way out of the classroom. "Oh great, we've only been back to school a few days and he's already giving us a test."

Charles overheard him and chuckled under his breath. Then he walked over to his desk and picked up a huge stack of mail. Thumbing through the pile, he spotted a small parcel and immediately checked the return address.

STING OF THE SEER

PROFESSOR JEREMY THOMPSON
666 BACKWORDS DRIVE
NEW ORLEANS, LOUISIANA XXXXX

Charles frowned after seeing the name on the box and then chucked the small package into the trash. "I'm not interested in anything you have to say, Jeremy."

Melissa, Charles' younger sister and one of his students, grabbed her schoolbooks and hurried over to her brother. She punched him in the arm and whined, "Come on, bro, I'm hungry, take me to lunch."

Charles didn't bother to look up at her as he continued browsing through the stack of mail. He replied unemotionally, "In a minute."

Melissa laid her schoolbooks down on her brother's desk and noticed the box lying on top of a pile of paper wads in the trash. Curious, she picked it up and said, "What's this?"

He answered back in a nasty mood, "Garbage."

Reading the name on the package, she replied excitedly, "It's from Jeremy. Aren't you going to open it?"

"No."

"Why not?"

"Because I don't want to."

"Fine, then I'll open it."

Melissa opened the box and discovered a newspaper wrapped tightly around a hidden object. She immediately removed the wrapping to uncover a paperback titled, *Sting of the Seer*, by Charter Road.

When she tried to hand the book to her brother, he pushed it away and said harshly, "No thanks! I'm not interested."

"Come on, Charles, aren't you the least bit curious why Jeremy sent you this book?"

"No. As far as I'm concerned, Jeremy is a missing link."

Melissa leaned against the desk, taking a moment to reflect on the past. "I used to have such a crush on him. I think it was his funny sense of humor that attracted me to him. Remember what you did when you found out I liked him?"

"Don't remind me."

"You were so worried about my virtue that you bought me a chastity belt for my sixteenth birthday."

Melissa set the book down on the desk and doubled over laughing.

Charles inquired sternly, "Are you finished yet?"

She let out another belly full of chuckles and said, "I'm sorry, Charles. I didn't mean to laugh at you. I think I got it all out now, pahahahahahah."

Charles was not amused by all her cackling. He stroked his clean-shaven cheek agitatedly and frowned at his sister who was still laughing at his expense.

Melissa knew Charles was getting upset with her. So she squeezed her lips tightly trying to hold in the laughter. But before she knew it, another snicker burst out of her mouth, heeheeheeheehee. Sorry, Charles, I couldn't help it. Those giggle bubbles just slipped out, honest."

Melissa doubled over laughing again.

Charles rolled his sullen eyes at her immaturity. Not wanting to lose his temper, he quickly redirected his thoughts to opening the mail."

Melissa felt remorseful she had pricked her brother's pride and wanted desperately to get back into his good graces. She lifted his chin up and stared into his emerald green eyes. "Come on, Charles, don't be mad at me. When you gave me that ridiculous gift on my birthday, I admit, I thought you'd lost your marbles. But I want you to know something, I did get the message."

"You did, huh. Well it might interest you to know that Jeremy's back in town."

"He is?"

"Yeah; look at the return address."

"That's news to me. Last I heard he quit his job about six months ago to search for some lost treasure in Egypt."

"He didn't quit his job. He was fired."

Charles snatched the newspaper out of her hand and glanced at the headline: DON'T LET THIS HAPPEN TO YOU.

"Why? He was a good teacher."

He slammed the paper down on his desk and said angrily, "That turned bad!"

"Jeremy? I don't believe it."

"It's true. He even admitted to the Dean that he went beyond the philosophical teachings on literature when he tried to brainwash his students into believing they could actually become lords of flies."

Melissa laughed and said, "You're not serious?"

"I told you he was nuts."

"Now where would he get a crazy idea like that?"

"Out of one of those stupid occult books that deceive people into believing they can become a god."

Charles walked over to the bookshelf and removed a paperback titled, *Baal-zebub, Lord of the Flies*, and handed it to Melissa.

"Apparently, after the nutty professor read about this mystical god, he wanted to become like him. So he started praying to it. A month later, he received a map in the mail accompanied with a note telling him to go to Egypt…alone, and he would receive further instructions. I can't believe the stupid fool actually went thinking it was a sign from god."

She giggled, "You're kidding me right?"

"I wish I was."

"Couldn't you talk him out of it?"

"No. You know how stubborn he is. He wouldn't listen to anything I had to say. He was going no matter what."

Charles took the occult book from Melissa and smacked it against the palm of his hand. Gritting his teeth out of anger, he said, "You know what else really irks me?"

"What?"

"It didn't bother Jeremy that this so-called Egyptian treasure map was sent to him anonymously. He didn't even question it. How blind can he be?"

"The map was written in Egyptian—was it authentic?"

"I guess. He wouldn't let me examine it other than telling me it was inscribed in goat skin."

"I didn't know Jeremy could read hieroglyphics."

"Yeah, we both studied ancient languages when we were in college."

"Why?"

"Because we wanted to get close to a couple of good-looking babes, that's why."

"And who talked you into that, Jeremy?"

Charles laughed and said, "Yeah. Can you believe it? He even talked me into taking a full semester of ballet just to get a date with this gorgeous redhead named, Edna. The only problem is I never got a date with either girl. It was always Jeremy who got the chicks."

She patted him on the back and said teasingly, "You poor baby."

"No. I wouldn't say that. I believe it's because God wanted me to save myself for the woman he picked out for me. You know...my destiny."

Melissa smiled fondly and said, "Yeah. I think so too."

Staring back at the cover of the occult book, Charles' heart instantly embellished with detestation. "This stinks!"

He angrily flung the book across the room and grumbled, "And people wonder what's wrong with our youth today when this garbage is allowed to be taught in school."

Feeling overwhelmed with curiosity, Charles nonchalantly glanced at the book on his desk.

Melissa elbowed her brother and said, "Go on, Charles, swallow your pride and pick it up. You know you're dying to find out why Jeremy sent you that book."

Charles set the stack of mail down on his desk and then opened the cover of the book. After seeing a picture drawn in black ink, he said, "What the hell is that?"

Melissa instantly gave Charles a stern look.

"What?"

"Your choice of words."

"What about it?"

"You said the "h" word again."

"So, it's in the Bible."

"You didn't say it in that context. You said it as a euphemism, and God doesn't want us going around offending people. He told us to choose our words wisely. Why let evil use your voice box as a litter box?"

"All right, all right, I'll work on it. Rome wasn't built in a day."

Charles showed Melissa the drawing inside the cover and said, "So what do you think it is?"

Melissa stared intently at the depiction and then spun the book around to read all the letters in the circle. "It looks like a ring of bee flies formed together to spell out the words, *HELP ME.*"

Destiny walked up to Charles and said mysteriously, "Your friend's in trouble. He needs your help."

Charles turned around and was startled to see Destiny standing there. He thought she had left the classroom. As he gazed into her sparkling sea blue eyes, he became speechless.

Destiny went on to say, "A disembodied evil spirit that calls itself Baal-zebub is slowly taking over Jeremy's mind. It was imprisoned in the Middle East until a warlock from New Orleans helped it escape. Then a year ago, the spirit was exorcised out of the warlock and put back into a prison in the desert."

"And now it escaped again with the help of Jeremy," Melissa said disappointedly.

Destiny nodded.

"Why the desert?" asked Melissa.

"The desert is merely symbolical for the condition of nomadic souls apart from God, a virtual wasteland. These lost souls continually search for something to quench their thirst in order to have rest."

Destiny held up the *Holy Bible* in her hand and said, "But without the spiritual waters of God, they'll never find it."

Melissa felt grieved thinking about all the people who didn't know Jesus. She knew Destiny was right. Jesus is the only one who can gratify the human soul. Everyone without Him will try to fill his or her emptiness with all sorts of wicked things.

"Why did this particular spirit pick Jeremy?" queried Melissa.

"Because Jeremy desired him."

"Oh," she replied sorrowfully.

"I heard from the Pastor that demonic rulers are very territorial. Is that why the dark lord brought Jeremy back here?" inquired Melissa.

"I'm not sure."

Melissa elbowed Charles and said in a barely audible voice, "Are you listening to her?"

"Huh? What?"

"I said are you listening to her?"

Charles whispered back, "To be honest, no; I took one look in her eyes and got lost at sea."

Melissa rolled her eyes and said annoyingly, "Oh brother."

Destiny soon became aware of Charles' fascination with her so she immediately walked away.

Soon as she left the room, the enchanted Professor hit his chest several times with his fist and blurted out, "Mercy, be still my heart. She is so beautiful."

"Forget it lover boy. She's in love with someone else."

"She is huh?"

Melissa nodded.

"Then I guess I'll have to make her forget all about him, won't I?" he arrogantly replied.

She giggled teasingly.

"What are you laughing at?"

"You; you could never compete with Him."

"And why not?"

Melissa laughed so hard she started coughing. "Because you'd have to compete with the almighty God; she's sworn to celibacy."

Charles took a quick peek at Destiny who was out in the hallway talking to her friends. "You mean no man can ever touch that beautiful creature?"

Melissa grinned smugly and shook her head. "Nope, and it's not like you were making any points with her today in class anyway."

Charles replied remorsefully, "Oh yeah, I didn't mean to call her out like that. It's just that I get so upset with her. She doesn't seem to care anything about Entomology, and that's something I'm very passionate about."

"Look at the pot calling the kettle black. Destiny's very passionate about the Word of God are you?"

Charles felt convicted he had neglected to read his Bible for quite some time and immediately turned away. After a few moments of thinking quietly to himself, he glanced down at the words inside the cover of the book and queried, "How did she know Baal-zebub was cast out of that warlock?"

"I don't know. Destiny's a *Seer*. Maybe God revealed some things to her when I asked her to pray for Jeremy."

Charles looked at the title on the cover of the book and said, "A *Seer*? You mean a *Prophetess*?"

"Yes, silly. If you'd come to church once in awhile, you'd know that."

"I go to church," he replied defensively.

"Charles, who are you kidding? The last time you went to church was almost two years ago."

"Has it really been that long?"

"Yes, and you know God forbids us to forsake the gathering of the saints. You taught me that when I was little. I just don't know how you can teach me one thing and do another."

Charles glanced back at Destiny while nervously flipping through the pages of the book. "So she goes to our church, huh?"

"Not wanting to rain on your parade but aren't you a little old for her?"

"No," he replied indignantly.

She snickered under her breath and said, "Talk about robbing the cradle. Charles, Destiny's my age, she's twenty-one. That makes her fourteen years younger than you are."

"So!"

"So? What happened to that speech you gave me when I was fifteen?"

"What speech?"

"You know what speech. 'Jeremy's way too old for you Melissa. You need to find someone more your own age.'"

"Oh, well, that was different. I was just trying to protect your reputation."

"That is so hypocritical."

"Melissa, do you still have feelings for Jeremy?"

"Oh please, Charles, I think I've matured since then."

"Does that mean you don't?"

"Give me a break, the guy has love affairs at the drop of a hat and doesn't care anything about Jesus. Why would I want him?"

"That's good. Then I don't have to buy you another chastity belt for your next birthday, hahahahahaha."

"Ha-ha-ha-ha, you don't have to worry about me, Charles. I intend to have my virginity intact on my wedding night."

He kissed his sister on the right cheek and said, "Good girl. Oh, by the way, what's with all the idiomatic expressions lately?"

"What do you mean?"

"You know, saying things like, 'Robbing the cradle, pot calling the kettle black,' and my all time favorite you now use when you're correcting me, 'Put that in your pipe and smoke it.'"

Melissa giggled, "It's your own fault. You're the one who bought me that book on idioms and told me to read it."

"That's only because you didn't understand some of the expressions I was using. I didn't know I was going to turn you into an idiom queen. I tell you what, since you love to read so much, why don't you read one of my psychology books instead? I got piles in my study."

"I always wondered why you bought all those books until I found out Jeremy had schizophrenia."

"How did you know about that?" he said worriedly.

"I saw the pills in his overnight bag when he stayed at our house one night."

"Oh. I was hoping I could find a miracle in one of the books that could help Jeremy. But I never found it," he said sorrowfully.

"That's because you weren't looking in the right book."

Melissa walked over to the book shelf and pulled out the *Holy Bible*. She blew the dust off the top of the cover and then handed it to Charles.

Charles took the Bible from her and laid it down on his desk. He said anxiously, "Melissa, please don't tell Jeremy you know he's schizophrenic. If he found out you knew it would crush him."

"Charles, I love Jeremy like a brother. I would never do anything to hurt him. Don't worry your secret is safe with me. How long has he been battling the psychotic disorder?"

"He's had schizophrenia for about two years now. I felt sorry for him when he first got it. The mental illness really got him down until he learned to live with it. He didn't want people to treat him like he was some sort of freak so he never told a soul except me and his doctor."

Melissa put her hand on her brother's shoulder and tried to reason with him. "Charles, you've been a good friend to Jeremy. Don't shut him out of your heart now just because he made a stupid mistake."

Charles ignored her request by turning the pages in the book. While thumbing his way to the middle of the novel, he spotted a piece of paper stuck to the page. "What in the world?"

Seeing her brother's dazed expression as he stared at the paper, Melissa asked apprehensively, "What is that?"

Charles carefully examined the sticky paper and said, "It looks like flypaper with another message from Jeremy."

"What does it say?"

"From what I can ascertain, these pictures of bee flies spell out the words, BAAL-ZEBUB and BEELZEBUB."

"Beelzebub? Isn't that another name for...."

Suddenly, a stinkbug fell out of the book and onto Charles' desk.

Melissa jumped back screaming, "Aaaaaagh, what is that thing?"

"It's a stinkbug."

Melissa plugged her nose and loudly protested in a distorted voice, "That stink would bug anybody. Get rid of it!"

Charles coughed from the smell secreted by the insect and then quickly grabbed a jar off the shelf. Using the newspaper on his desk, he scraped the bug into the jar. "Oh man, I've never known a stinkbug to emit that strong an odor before."

"I don't know about you, but I'm getting out of here. I'll wait for you at the diner."

He looked at his wristwatch and said, "Sis, give me about five minutes to clean up, okay."

"All right, but hurry up, I'm starving."

7

Lightning flashed across the dark storm-clouded sky, exposing an old abandoned shack at the edge of the Louisiana marshland. Shortly afterward, thunder rumbled through the heavens and heavy rains began to pour. The familiar sounds created by crickets and bullfrogs pierced the stillness of the night as they echoed through the quagmire.

Through the window of the small shack, you could see Jeremy leaning on a table next to an old kerosene lamp. He was busy trying to steady his quivering hand in order to write a message inside the cover of a paperback. As he pressed the tip of the feather pen to the page, the black ink flowed out and miraculously formed into a stinkbug. Feeling inundated with tension, he brushed the bug off the table and bellowed into the air. "Stop it!"

Jeremy dipped the pen back into the inkwell and attempted to write a second time. When the ink formed into another stinkbug, he quickly lost patience and shouted heatedly, "No! You will not stop me!"

All at once, the Professor started hacking and choking on the powerful stench emitted by the stinkbugs. Covering his nose and mouth with the handkerchief, he tried to write again. Only this time, the ink poured out of the pen and rapidly formed into hundreds of stinkbugs that scrambled around on the table forming themselves into words: *I WOULD HAVE LEFT YOU AT THAT NICE COVEN IN THE CITY BUT YOU TRICKED ONE OF MY WITCHES INTO MAILING A BOOK FOR YOU.*

Jeremy's eyes widened as his heart flooded with fear.
YES, JEREMY, I KNOW ALL ABOUT THE BOOK.
He cried out, "What did you do to her?"
I KILLED HER.
Baal-zebub laughed insanely.
"Noooooo!" he screamed in a fit of rage.

Jumping up out of his seat, he started smacking the bugs off the table like a madman. After thoroughly exhausting himself, he collapsed back in his chair and started sobbing heavily. "How could you do that? She was my friend."

The stinkbugs reappeared on the table spelling words: YOU WASTED YOUR TIME. CHARLES WON'T HELP YOU. HE THINKS YOU'RE NUTS.

The Professor shouted to the top of his lungs, "Liar!"

Tired of being chained to fear, Jeremy sprung to his feet and made a mad dash for the door. But the moment he tried to run outside, he slammed into an invisible barrier and landed on his derriere.

Baal-zebub's deep monotonic laughter flooded the room.

Covering his ears, Jeremy shouted, "You can't keep me here!"

Determined to escape, the Professor got back up and tried it again, only to be knocked down by the same unseen force.

Baal-zebub laughed uncontrollably as the creaky cabin door slowly closed.

The Professor stared defiantly at the little bugs crawling on the table and shook his head in disgust. Then he looked towards the open window with great anticipation. Hurrying fast as he could, he climbed out the casement only to find himself back in the same room.

The stinkbugs rapidly spelled the words: HAHAHAHA.

Upon seeing the words, Jeremy knocked the bugs back off the table and shouted furiously, "You make me sick!"

He flopped down in his chair still feeling bad tempered and wiped the perspiration from his forehead. Directly afterward, he felt something crawling on his abdominal area and squealed unpleasantly, "Ugh! What is that?"

He immediately lifted his shirt to see what it was and saw stinkbugs spelling out words: SEER, SPEAK FOR ME!

Jeremy tried brushing the nasty little bugs off his tummy while responding to the creature's demand. "No. I will not speak for you. You're not the voice of God. You're the voice of an idiot. Now get off me!"

When the Professor realized he couldn't remove any of the phantom bugs from his stomach, no matter how hard he tried, he said humorously, "I've heard of people taking their work home with them, but this is ridiculous. Heeheehee."

Unfortunately, his laughter was short lived when he felt searing pain on his belly. Checking his tummy, he noticed the stinkbugs had vanished without a trace. However, they made a lasting impression by branding the message into his flesh. Infuriated by what the Dragonfly did to him, he glared around the empty room and hollered, "I hope that's not permanent, and the answer is still no!"

The instant he finished giving his resounding refusal the ghostly Dragonfly appeared across the room, transmitting a message into Jeremy's mind that made him feel haughty.

YOU WILL LEARN TO OBEY ME.

Highly annoyed by the beast's demands, the Professor scoffed at the creature by shouting spitefully, "Never! Can't you get that through your stupid teensy-fly brain? I'm sick of your manure!"

The Dragonfly protested profoundly at the human's insubordination by screaming like a banshee and then started coming towards him. Jeremy swallowed hard trying not to look scared as the creature got closer to his face. "Ugh, get your bad breath out of my face."

The Professor instinctively grabbed a chair off the floor and threw it at the oversized insect. "Get away from me!"

The cantankerous Dragonfly laughed at the rowdy human while dodging each object he threw. Then the behemoth released an ear-piercing hum that summoned thousands of ghostly bee flies. As the insects swarmed in through the open window, Jeremy covered his ears to protect them from their intense droning, which was almost deafening to his eardrums.

When the Professor realized the livid flies were forming themselves into a huge wall around him, he shut his eyes tightly and didn't dare move a muscle. He didn't want to go through the same nightmare he had experienced in the cave. Real or imagined, the stinger of that horrible night was still stuck in his mind.

Not being able to trust his own eyes anymore, Jeremy felt relatively safe with them closed. He figured with his eyes shut, his soul would be protected from seeing the Dragonfly's sadistic expression. But much to his surprise, the beast's intimidating words still formed inside his mind.

TEACH HIM A LESSON HE WILL NEVER FORGET.

The Professor cringed at the scorn in the beast's voice. When he heard a loud whistle, his eyes shot open, and he screamed in great anguish, "No! Not again!"

All at once, a thousand bee flies from the horde around him descended on his body. Jeremy slowly dropped to his knees with tears streaming down his olive-colored cheeks, whimpering with uncertainty, "This can't be happening. Bee flies can't sting people."

The buzzing bee flies' mischievous spirits quickly spelled out the words: *THEN WHY ARE YOU SCREAMING?*

Baal-zebub chuckled maliciously.

Jeremy soon reached his breaking point and became quite animated. He cried out frantically, "Somebody help me, please! Help me! Please, somebody, help me! Please help me!"

Regrettably, no human was around to hear his disparaging cries, and a few minutes later, he was too exhausted to fight. His body was racked with pain from hundreds of bee stings, and his breathing was strained. He appeared almost lifeless lying on the floor on his back, staring hypnotically at the angry bee flies circling overhead.

The buzzing bee flies spelled out the words: WHAT ARE YOU THINKING, HUMAN?

Jeremy failed to answer the question. He was now unable to see or hear the humming of the words, because his face had swollen six times its normal size.

When the Dragonfly realized that Jeremy was completely incoherent, it removed his chains of affliction and drummed the question into his head again.

WHAT ARE YOU THINKING HUMAN?

Jeremy blinked several times to empty the tears out of his eyes and then read the message. After he'd finished, he grinned wickedly and decided to mock the evil creature again by stating, "The fact that you do not know proves you are the son of darkness, for a real God would know what I was thinking."

IF YOU CAN STILL THINK FOR YOURSELF, HUMAN, YOU ARE NOT DEAD ENOUGH FOR ME.

Once more, the Dragonfly whistled, and the angry bee flies covered the Professor's body, stinging him over and over again. Not being able to withstand the severe pain, he started gnashing his teeth. "What are you?"

PURE EVIL! I HAVE ALWAYS BEEN AND ALWAYS WILL BE.

The thought of being tormented by evil for all eternity terrified Jeremy's soul. He screamed so loud he could be heard from miles away. "Noooooooooo!"

After an hour of stinging him unmercifully with his demonic thoughts, the Dragonfly whistled again, and the bee flies withdrew.

ARE YOU READY TO OBEY ME, HUMAN?

Jeremy stridently voiced his hostility after listening intently to the riveting made by the loud-mouthed bullfrogs outside the opened window. "Go ahead sting me to death! See if I care. Because I'd rather croak than speak for you, hahahahaha."

Seeking revenge, the Professor decided to reveal the secret the witch confided in him. "And I'm sure that's exactly how the warlock priest felt years ago when he had you exorcised. I imagine he got so sick of your voice he would have done anything to bury it back into the dust."

The beast's voice roared angrily throughout the shack.

Jeremy laughed at the Dragonfly with a sense of superiority. "That's right; the witch you killed told me all about how one of your high priests betrayed you after his heart was touched by the voice of Jesus. She said it happened right after he read a book given to him by a Christian seer he met at a dance studio. It was the same book the witch gave me, only I never got around to reading it. Instead, I decided to use the book to help me escape by sending a message in it to Charles. What was in that book that you were so afraid of?"

Jeremy mulled it over in his mind, and then his eyes widened with revelation. He blurted out in a voice of distress, "Oh no, the witch read that book. That's why you had her killed. You were afraid she might eventually turn to love Jesus' voice too."

The Dragonfly wailed in a fit of rage as the Professor's heart embraced the truth.

HUMAN, YOU WILL LEARN TO RESPECT ME, OR BITE THE DUST!

All of a sudden, the floor turned into quicksand. Feeling his feet slipping out from under him, he shouted fearfully, "What's going on here? What are you doing? Stop! Stop I said!"

Jeremy screamed hysterically while trying to grab a hold of anything he could get his hands on. "Nooooo! Somebody, help me, please! I don't want to die! Please, somebody help me!"

After sinking deeper and deeper into the abyss of sand, Jeremy began to hear the tune of the *Sandman* lulling him to sleep. Then an hourglass appeared in front of him with only a few grains of sand left at the top.

TIME FLIES WHEN YOU'RE HAVING FUN.

Baal-zebub laughed cruelly.

Jeremy started crying and whimpering like a baby while trying to wipe the dust out of his eyes. "Please, don't put me to sleep. If I die, I might not ever wake up again. Please, I don't know of any gods who can wake up the dead except Charles' God, and I don't even know if Jesus really exists."

Fearfully watching the remaining sands of his life slowly pass through the hourglass, he lost hope and began to panic. "No! Please, my time can't be up! Charles, help me, I'm afraid! I don't know what's going to happen to me after I die. Please help me!"

A moment later, Jeremy's insane ravings were silenced, and he slowly disappeared beneath the dust.

8

The Professor heard the precious sound of time ticking away as he miraculously appeared back on the floor choking and wheezing for air. Feeling like his lungs were going to explode, he rolled off his back and on to his side. He spit the dust out of his mouth and started inhaling some deep breaths. After coughing several times, he slowly felt his strength coming back.

Now he knew exactly how his friend Charles had felt when he was drowning in the cold murky waters sixteen years earlier. Like Charles, Jeremy had learned a very valuable lesson. The breath of life is a gift from God and not to be taken lightly. He also knew the voice of evil was suffocating his soul to death, but he didn't know how to stop it.

While spitting more dust out of his mouth, Jeremy eyed another message on the wall spelled by the bee flies.

WHAT'S THE MATTER, JEREMY? DID YOU BITE OFF MORE THAN YOU COULD CHEW? HOW DID YOU LIKE BEING BURIED ALIVE? YOU DON'T THINK IT'S SO FUNNY NOW DO YOU?

Jeremy coughed on the dust in his throat and then asserted his bitterness aggressively. "You should have left me to die, because I'm not going to help you."

AFTER THE DUST CLEARS FROM YOUR HEAD, YOU'LL SEE THINGS MY WAY.

Wiping the sandy tears from his eyes, he shouted hatefully, "Never!"

The Dragonfly roared angrily at his response and then drummed another message into his head.

SEER, IF YOU WILL NOT SPEAK FOR ME THEN MY THOUGHTS WILL CONTINUE TO STING YOU. YOU WILL LONG FOR DEATH, BUT YOU WILL NOT SEE IT.

When the sound of a loud whistle pierced his left eardrum, he queried fearfully, "What are you going to do?"

Before Jeremy had a chance to move a muscle, the bee flies covered him and continued the stinging ritual. Dropping to the floor, he blubbered pitiably, "Please don't hurt me anymore. Please. Why can't you just leave me alone? Why?"

Several hours later after numerous attacks that didn't lead to death, he thought, *Will this torment ever end?*

Then he felt a sticky wetness beneath him. He looked down and was mortified to see himself lying in a pool of his own blood. He sobbed, "Ugh, that's so gross."

Scrunching his eyes tightly, Jeremy moaned, "I think I'm going to be sick."

Instantly, he turned pale as a ghost and vomited acid out of his empty stomach. Right before he passed out, he swatted at the imaginary silver flies circling above his head.

The Professor had lain unconscious for about an hour before being awakened by the sound of whistling wind and shudders banging back and forth outside the window. Still groggy, he slowly opened his blurry eyes and glanced over at the window. Gripping the sides of his head, he moaned, "Ooooooh! I feel like there's a bunch of bees buzzing around inside my head."

The next moment, he heard a helicopter flying overhead and said, "A helicopter? Where am I?"

Soon as he saw the bee flies crawling all over his body and the puddle of blood on the floor, he groaned miserably, "Ugh! Now I know why I heard a helicopter, because I need to be rescued from hell."

The bee flies continued stinging the half-crazed Professor sporadically until around midnight. The extreme pain he was experiencing kept making him feel nauseous and induced repeated bouts of dry heaves. By that time, Jeremy was now humbled to the point of groveling and sniveled miserably, "Please stop. Please. I'll do anything you want. Just don't hurt me anymore, please."

The very next moment, the Professor heard a loud whistle, and the thoughts of an evil raspy voice that sounded like it was coming from inside a tomb.

RELEASE HIM.

The flies immediately obeyed and pulled back.

The Professor was rigid with fear and scrunched his eyes tightly. He wasn't sure if the voice inside his head was real or only another delusion created out of his schizophrenic mind.

I KNEW YOU WOULD GIVE IN.

Jeremy meditated on the beast's thoughts for a moment with his eyes still closed. He whispered under his breath, "Give in? So that's what "cave time" meant. The lord of flies knew it was just a matter of time before he would get me to cave in, and I would bury my own conscience."

"It's my own fault. I desired to be like this lord. I wanted the power to rule over the entire insect empire; my own special army that would outnumber the human kingdom by more than a billion to one. I would be their General, and they would have to obey my every command."

He shook his head feeling sorry for himself and continued rambling, "What an idiot! Charles warned me not to dabble in the occult. He practically drew me a map, but I was too stupid to listen. He said, 'There can only be one God, Jeremy.'"

After the Professor finished having a pity party, he sensed a dead silence in the room. He gradually opened one eye and then the other while cautiously looking around for any signs of danger. When he noticed all the insects were gone, as well as his wounds and the blood on the floor, he heaved a huge sigh of relief. Thinking the pandemonium was finally over, he chuckled, "It was all just another stupid illusion."

Unfortunately, his blissful emotions soon turned melancholy when he heard heavy breathing directly behind him. He said in a voice of panic, "Oh no, please, don't let it be that deranged, over-sized, green bug thing that thinks it's a dragon."

The shaky Professor slowly turned around to see who it was. The instant he saw the Dragonfly's evil smirking face staring back at him, he screamed to the top of his lungs, "Aaaaaaaagh, not you again!"

Leaping to his feet, he bolted for the door fast as he could. When he turned around and saw the Dragonfly chasing after him, he grabbed the kerosene lamp off the table and threw it at the hideous beast. The moment the lantern hit the floor it exploded into a huge inferno.

The Professor shouted belligerently at the undaunted Dragonfly who was hovering within the flames. "I hate you! I hate you!"

The beast quickly communicated its demonic thoughts to the human's mind.

YOU DON'T HATE ME JEREMY. AFTER ALL, I WAS THE ONE WHO PLANTED THE PICTURES OF ME IN YOUR HEART SO YOU COULD LOVE ME LIKE ALL THE OTHER PRIESTS BEFORE YOU. IT WAS THE ONLY WAY I COULD GET YOU TO UNBURY MY VOICE.

Jeremy snapped sharply, "What are you talking about? When I unburied your unholy bible out of the sand, there was nothing in it but dust."

DID YOU ACTUALLY THINK YOU'D FIND MY WORDS OUTSIDE OF YOU? MY EVIL THOUGHTS WENT INTO YOUR HEART THE MOMENT YOU BELIEVED IN ME. YOU OPENED THE DOOR AND LET ME IN.

"You devil, you lied to me. You promised me the power to become a son of God."

MY SON, YOU POSSESSED MY POWERS THE DAY YOU WERE BORN.

He curled his lip in disgust and said, "I'm not your son."

I AM THE GOD OF THIS WORLD, THE FATHER OF ALL LIES. SO TELL ME, HUMAN, HOW MANY LIES HAVE YOU TOLD IN YOUR LIFETIME? TOO MANY TO COUNT I IMAGINE. SINCE YOU LIKE TO CONTROL THE MINDS OF OTHERS BY MAKING THEM BELIEVE IN SOMETHING THAT ISN'T TRUE, DOES THAT NOT MAKE YOU MY SON?

Jeremy sneered at the hellacious creature and said distastefully, "I don't want to be like you. You bug me."

OH REALLY?

"Yeah, and I'm going to start calling you, "Bug Dragon," since you won't quit bugging me. So tell me, Bug Dragon, why did you put a note warning me about evil and a *Holy Bible* in the treasure box too? Isn't that a little out of character for somebody like you?"

YOU'RE LYING. I WOULD NEVER TEMPT YOU WITH ANYTHING HOLY.

Jeremy was puzzled by the beast's response. He mumbled to himself, "Did I imagine that too?"

9

When the Dragonfly failed to coax Jeremy into the flames, it decided to alter its form.

SINCE YOU DON'T LIKE MY CURRENT APPEARANCE, MAYBE I CAN FIND ONE THAT IS MORE APPEALING TO YOU.

All at once, the Dragonfly started changing itself into a glamorous dragon-lady.

Jeremy was mesmerized watching the metamorphosis. "That's amazing. The Bug Dragon appears to be metaphorical. It's using the power of suggestion to project vivid images into my mind.

SEER, I APPEARED THE MOMENT YOU TURNED YOUR HEART TO SEE MY VOICE.

"That's strange. Now I hear the creature's voice as clearly as I hear my own. Have I grown that accustomed to it?"

Staring longingly at the dragon-lady, Jeremy said, "I got to admit, her spirit is beautiful. And I love the sound of her Spanish accent. It's erotically appealing and hard to resist.

JEREMY, I BURN FOR YOU. GIVE YOUR SOUL TO ME, AND I'LL GRANT YOU THE DESIRES OF YOUR HEART: POWER TO RULE THE ENTIRE INSECT KINGDOM, UNENDING RICHES, AND SEXUAL FULFILLMENT BEYOND YOUR WILDEST DREAMS.

The Professor stared lustfully at the seductive flames, desiring all the things she said. But the instant he approached the flames, fear overcame him, and he pulled back.

I TOLD YOU, THE FIRE WON'T HURT YOU AS LONG AS YOU WORSHIP ME.

He replied in a whimper, "No, I can't do it. I'm afraid."
LET ME HELP YOU.
The seductress slowly started taking her clothes off.
COME TO ME, JEREMY, I BURN FOR YOU.
Gazing hypnotically at the huge flames, he shook his head vigorously.
I WON'T HURT YOU.
When the dragon-lady stripped all the way down to her birthday suit, the Professor turned away, whining pathetically, "Please, stop tempting me."
DON'T RESIST ME, JEREMY. I CAN MAKE YOU FEEL SO GOOD.
Sniffing the erotic aroma of her perfume, he looked back at her nakedness and thought, *Who is this mysterious creature of seduction anyway? Is she just another hallucination?*
Ogling her voluptuous body, he wiped the sweat from his brow and said suspiciously, "Why are you getting me hot?"
SIN HAS ITS PLEASURES, BUT IN ORDER TO BE BIRTHED, IT MUST HAVE HEAT. NOW COME TO ME.
Jeremy's philandering spirit made it virtually impossible for him to resist the temptation to commit fornication with her and eventually stepped into the flames.

After several moments of heavy breathing and passionate kissing, he opened his eyes and saw the seductress' beautiful face transforming into a hideous dragonfly's. Horrified by her appearance, he screamed bloody murder and pushed the dragon-lady away. "Aaaaaaagh! I've been kissing a devil!"

Baal-zebub laughed heartlessly as its evil spirit overpowered the weak-minded human. A few seconds later, Jeremy had a wicked grin on his face, and his eyes were glowing red. Even his clothes had miraculously changed into a black pinned-striped suit with a black rose pinned to the lapel. His hair was all slicked back, and he looked like a gangster back in the bootlegging days.

JEREMY, MY THOUGHTS WILL NEVER LEAVE YOU. WE ARE JOINED TOGETHER FOR AN ETERNITY.

Suddenly, a giant black ring with a huge black diamond appeared and slid over the top of him. Then it disappeared and reappeared on Jeremy's left index finger. As he stepped out of the flames, the voice inside his head changed to sound like his own.

I HAVE YOUR WHOLE LIFE MAPPED OUT FOR YOU.

The dark circles under Jeremy's eyes and the heavy perspiration dripping from his head, were a dead give away that he was very sick. Feeling weak-willed, he sat down at the table, mumbling under his breath, "I don't feel good."

AN EVIL HEART NEVER DOES.

Baal-zebub's unruly laughter boomed through the Professor's soul as if it were being heard over a loud speaker.

While communing with the evil spirit's thoughts, Jeremy queried, "What do you want me for anyway?"

I NEED YOU TO HELP ME STING GOD'S BODY TO DEATH.

"His body?"

THE CHURCH.

"Why?"

REVENGE.

"For what?"

FOR CHAINING ME TO A LIFE OF HELL.

"So that's why you're wearing those chains. You're bound for hell, hahahaha."

All of a sudden, the room was filled with music and jovial laughter. Jeremy slowly turned around and saw thirty poltergeists dressed up for the Mardi Gras. He asked in great surprise, "Where did they come from?"

DON'T YOU JUST LOVE THE MARDI GRAS? YOU CAN HIDE BEHIND A MASK, AND NOBODY KNOWS WHO YOU ARE.

Baal-zebub chuckled spitefully and then transformed into a dark ghostly image that looked exactly like Jeremy.

The Professor stared alarmingly at the evil spirited clone. "What's going on here? You look exactly like me, but as a dead spirit."

NO. YOU LOOK LIKE ME.

A theatrical mask of a dragonfly suddenly appeared on Jeremy's face, and he jumped a foot. He quickly yanked off the mask and stared blankly at the hideous disguise, muttering regretfully, "I don't know who I am anymore. Why are you doing this anyway? I'm not you, and you're not me."

YOU'RE WRONG, JEREMY. YOU'RE MY SON. YOU HAVE MY SHADY CHARACTER. YOU MIRROR MY SOUL. YOU CAN'T TAKE OFF THE MASK. IT'S THE PART YOU HAVE BEEN CHOSEN TO PLAY. IT'S YOUR DESTINY.

After listening to Baal-zebub's evil thoughts buzzing around inside his head, he replied unfeelingly, "Great."

When it got quiet in the room, Jeremy turned around and noticed the masqueraders had vanished unexpectedly. "Where did everybody go?"

THE PARTY'S OVER, JEREMY, IT'S TIME TO PAY THE PIPER.

The Professor answered back fearfully, "What is that supposed to mean?"

YOU'LL FIND OUT SOON ENOUGH.

Baal-zebub gawked at Jeremy without saying a word. Finally, when the Professor couldn't stand the clone staring at him anymore, he touched the side of his cheek and snapped edgily, "What? Why are you staring at me?"

YOU'RE GOING TO HELP ME TRAP A SEER.
"Why?"
BECAUSE GOD GAVE HER THE ABILITY TO SEE IN THE DARK PLACES, THAT'S WHY.
Jeremy smirked and said sarcastically, "To unmask you?"
The instant he mentioned the word, "*unmask,*" both the clone and the mask vanished simultaneously. The Professor laughed at the invisible ghost and then shouted into the air, "You're nothing without us, huh?"
IF I AM NOTHING, THEN WHY ARE YOU TALKING TO YOURSELF?
"Come on, admit it. You need us pathetic little humans to speak your words in order for your attributes to be seen."
The clone suddenly reappeared behind him.
SHUT UP!
Jeremy quickly spun around when he heard the clone behind him and chuckled, "I thought you wanted me to speak for you."
VERY FUNNY.
Jeremy sighed heavily and said, "Look, if this Seer's bugging you, why don't you just kill her?"
Baal-zebub growled irritably and then kicked one of the wooden chairs across the room.
BELIEVE ME, I'VE TRIED, BUT HER GOD ALWAYS PROTECTS HER.
"If her God is helping her, what can we do about it?"
Baal-zebub looked up for a moment and jeered at God.
DESTINY HAS A STINGER EMBEDDED IN HER FLESH.
"A stinger, what does that mean?"
IT'S A HUMAN WEAKNESS CALLED PRIDE. ALL HUMANS HAVE IT.

"So what are you going to do?"

I'M GOING TO PRICK HER PRIDE UNTIL SHE DRIVES THE VOICE OF GOD BACK INTO THE WILDERNESS, HAHAHAHA.

"How do you know so much about human weaknesses anyway?"

BECAUSE I PUT THEM THERE; I WAS ONCE INTIMATE WITH DESTINY UNTIL SHE REJECTED ME FOR HIM. I KNOW HER VERY WELL.

"Him, you mean Jesus?"

IF YOU MENTION THAT NAME AGAIN IN MY UNHOLY PRESENCE, I WILL INFLICT SO MUCH PAIN ON YOU THAT YOU WILL CURSE THE DAY YOU WERE BORN.

"All right, all right, don't get so touchy. I didn't know I was dealing with a jealous god."

SO IS HE. HE'D DO ANYTHING FOR HER.

"I heard He even sacrificed His life for the church."

IF YOU BELIEVE THAT, YOU'LL BELIEVE ANYTHING. I SUGGEST YOU STOP LISTENING TO CHARLES AND HIS ENDLESS FANTASIES AND START LISTENING TO ME. I AM THE VOICE OF GOD.

10

Jeremy squealed with fright when a projection of Destiny suddenly appeared in the room.

RELAX, IT'S ONLY AN ILLUSION.

He put his hand over his rapidly beating heart and sighed in relief. "Oh, it seems so real."

The Professor peered suspiciously at her projected image and said, "Wait a minute, she looks familiar. Where have I seen her before? Oh my goodness, she's the seer the witch told me about, the one that called upon her God to have you exorcised. The witch showed me her picture in a magazine article about rich heiresses. Now it all makes sense. You want revenge against her because she had your voice buried out in the desert. Hahahaha."

SHUT UP!

"I wish you'd make up your mind. Do you want me to speak for you, or do you want me to shut up? I can't do both."

As Jeremy continued watching the projected image of Destiny, he saw her running in slow motion through a beautiful forest, holding a thorn-less, blood-red rose in her right hand. Sunlight beamed through the woodlands as a variety of beautifully-colored butterflies hovered around her head. The young beauty, dressed in all white, laughed like an innocent child the moment a monarch butterfly landed on her right index finger.

She gently touched one of the wings on the butterfly with her fingertip and whispered, "Lord Jesus, I believe that everything you created is able to teach us something about you, like the complete metamorphosis of the butterfly. You taught me that its miraculous transformation is similar to the way the human mind is gradually transformed after receiving your Holy Spirit. The ugly wormy part of us that desires to sin is slowly done away with as the beauty of your soul takes over our thoughts."

"What is she talking about?" queried Jeremy.

WHO CARES, SHE'S CRAZY.

"Uh-huh, you mean crazy about her God. Boy, I wish she was crazy about me. My goodness, she's gorgeous."

YOU WON'T WANT HER AFTER YOU HEAR HER SPEAK.

Jeremy watched the butterfly on Destiny's finger flutter away. As he continued to gaze longingly at her beauty, he didn't understand the incredible joy she possessed. He said softly, "She seems so happy."

HOW CAN SHE BE WITHOUT ME?

Destiny stopped for a moment to admire the rays of light. Her eyes glinted while talking passionately to Jesus. "I remember what you said to me once, 'What kind of flower does God give to one He's lifting up?'"

She sniffed the aroma of the rose and said with a big smile, "A rose."

Destiny gently stroked the delicate petals on the flower until a huge hand of light appeared and lifted her high into the air. The Australian beauty was awestruck by her Lord's presence and said lovingly, "All the roses in the world couldn't lift you higher than you are right now."

The hand gently set her back down on the ground and dematerialized.

Jeremy said frustratingly, "I don't understand a word she's saying. It's like her brains are in la-la land or something."

After watching her for several moments, the Professor became doubtful of Baal-zebub's plan and said smugly, "I don't think you're going to be able to turn her against her God."

YOU'LL SEE; AND AFTER I DO, THE HOLY GHOST WILL BURN WITH JEALOUSY AS HE WATCHES HER CLIMB INTO THE BED OF MY THOUGHTS TO LOVE ME.

Jeremy replied sarcastically, "This I got to see."

DON'T WORRY. AFTER MY THOUGHTS HAVE WORMED THEIR WAY INTO THE BELLY OF HER SOUL, THEY'LL TRICK DESTINY INTO TURNING AGAINST HIS CHURCH. THE MOMENT SHE GETS REVENGE, I'LL REMIND HER THAT HER BELOVED'S HEART IS IN THE BODY....

The Professor cut in and said, "And by stinging the church, she hurts the heart of her God."

EXACTLY! AFTER SHE REALIZES WHAT SHE'S DONE, THE GUILT WILL BEAT THE ROSE OF HER HEART UNTIL EVERY PETAL FALLS OFF, HAHAHAHA.

Tears of joy streamed down Destiny's face as she continued talking to God. "Lord Jesus, I love to hear your voice. Your words are a fire in my soul burning to be spoken. You're an awesome God, my beloved. I don't want to ever lose you."

At that moment, a *Holy Bible* appeared in her hands. "Seer, always remember you have my thoughts living inside you. I have put them there to help you obey my voice."

While Jesus continued talking, His Holy Spirit materialized inside her body as a shimmering light. "You see me because you believe in me. My Spirit will never leave you. I am joined with you for an eternity, and no one can snatch you out of my hand."

Destiny's eyes sparkled as she felt the power of Jesus' words penetrating her soul. She loved the way his moral purity touched her heart. It was always there to protect her from evil.

Gazing up at the beautiful blue sky, she saw a huge diamond ring descending out of heaven. It slid over the top of her and then vanished, reappearing on her right index finger. Destiny stared at the white gem glittering in the light and said warmly, "The church is your bride, your gem, and the gates of hell will not prevail against her."

THAT'S WHAT YOU THINK.

Destiny hugged the Holy Bible to her heart and said passionately, "I love you Jesus…always."

Jeremy found her words absolutely repulsive and started gagging and coughing. He quickly covered his nose and mouth with his handkerchief and said, "Enough, before I throw up. My goodness, her breath is so bad I'd have to tape her mouth shut just to get near her. I don't understand how something so beautiful on the outside can be so ugly on the inside."

Baal-zebub sneered at Destiny and then bellowed bitterly.

THE FIRE IN YOUR SOUL FOR HIS HOLINESS SICKENS ME.

Baal-zebub looked up towards heaven and started shouting accusations at God.

YOU TURNED HER AGAINST ME BY TAKING AWAY HER EVIL SPIRIT.

The cloned creature kicked the end table over, still ramping and raving.

YOU MADE HER DIVORCE ME BY LIFTING HER OUT OF SIN. NOW SHE HATES ME.

All at once, objects in the room started crashing into the walls. Jeremy immediately crawled under the table to escape harm's way, grumbling under his breath, "My goodness and I thought I had a bad temper."

I HATE YOUR VOICE! I'M GOING TO SHUT YOU UP IF IT'S THE LAST THING I DO!

"How are you going to do that?"

Baal-zebub grinned wickedly at the projection of Destiny and then arrogantly shared his evil thoughts with Jeremy.

I'M GOING TO TRICK HIS CHURCH THAT HE FORMED OUT OF A SPECK OF DUST INTO BURYING HERSELF BACK INTO THE DIRT. FOR DUST SHE IS AND TO DUST SHE SHALL RETURN, HAHAHAHA.

AS FOR YOU DESTINY, I'M GOING TO GET YOU TO DESIRE ME AGAIN BY PUSHING ON YOUR STINGER. AFTER I PRICK YOUR PRIDE, YOU WILL ALLOW MY WORDS TO STROKE YOUR HEART UNTIL THEY IMPREGNATE YOU. THEN WHEN YOU GIVE BIRTH TO SIN, I'M GOING TO LOVE TORMENTING YOUR RIGHTEOUS SOUL AS IT ROLLS AROUND IN THE DIRT.

The projection of Destiny slowly faded way while Baal-zebub's taunting laughter flooded the room.

11

Suddenly, the walls were filled with ghostly honeycombs, guarded by thousands of buzzing bee flies.

Jeremy stared curiously at the walls and queried, "What's all this?"

CELLS FOR PRISONERS OF MY WILL.

Hearing a multitude of people screaming, the Professor guardedly peeked into one of the dark cells. "What's going to happen to them?"

DON'T YOU KNOW?

Jeremy shook his head.

THE STING OF SIN IS DEATH. SOONER OR LATER, EVERYONE HAS TO PAY THE PIPER.

Baal-zebub looked up towards heaven and growled.

UNLIKE SOMEONE I KNOW I HAVE NO MERCY. I BELIEVE YOU HUMANS CALL SUCH A PLACE, DEATH ROW.

Still peering into the same cell, the Professor queried nosily, "What's this guy in for?"

Baal-zebub smirked at the Professor and then took some black honey out of the comb.

THAT'S LIONELL PARKER, CELL NUMBER 166. HE LOVES THE TASTE OF PORNOGRAPHY.

Baal-zebub sucked the sticky substance off his ghostly finger and continued transmitting his immoral thoughts.

HE'S A MAN AFTER MY OWN HEART, HAHAHAHA.

"Why is he crying?"

BECAUSE HIS MARRIAGE DIED AFTER HIS WIFE FOUND OUT ABOUT IT.

"Oh. What about this poor soul?"

AH, THAT'S CHUCK KINGSLEY, CELL NUMBER 266. HE NEVER GOT WEANED OFF THE BOTTLE. ONE NIGHT, VERY SOON, THE BIG BABY GETS DRUNK AND BREAKS HIS STUPID NECK FALLING DOWN A FLIGHT OF STAIRS.

Baal-zebub sucked more black honey off his finger and laughed vindictively.

When Jeremy heard a female groaning as if she was in a great deal of pain, he peeped into the dark honeycomb and asked, "Who is she?"

THAT'S MARISSA PETERS, CELL NUMBER 366. SHE'S A DRUG ADDICT. SHE GOT ADDICTED TO PAIN KILLERS WHEN SHE INJURED HER BACK A FEW YEARS AGO. LATELY, SHE'S BEEN TAKING MORE AND MORE PILLS TRYING TO KILL HER PAIN. SHE KILLS IT ALRIGHT WITH AN OVERDOSE, HAHAHAHA.

"She has a heart attack and dies?"

YES.

"Good grief, aren't you the busy bee?"

YOU CAN CATCH MORE FLIES WITH HONEY, AND I KNOW EXACTLY WHAT KIND TO USE. WHAT CAN I SAY, THEY LOVE ME.

When Jeremy heard a man shouting obscenities at a little girl, he asked, "What about them? What are they in for?"

THAT'S GEORGE MACGREGOR AND HIS FIVE-YEAR-OLD DAUGHTER, JALINE, CELL NUMBER 466. HE LOVES THE TASTE OF VIOLENCE. THE BIG BULLY LOSES HIS TEMPER ONE NIGHT AND BEATS THE LITTLE GIRL TO DEATH. WHAT A SHAME. HE WINDS UP ON DEATH ROW, HAHAHAHA.

Jeremy sighed heavily and said, "I guess he paid the piper by receiving the same mercy he showed her. Then he walked across the room to look at another honeycomb. "Hey, this cell looks familiar."

IT SHOULD. CELL 566 IS A PLAYBOY AND LOVES TO FOOL AROUND. ONLY HE GOT CARELESS ONE NIGHT AND CONTRACTED AIDS.

He snickered and said, "What an idiot. Who is the poor dote?"

HIS NAME IS PROFESSOR...JEREMY...THOMPSON.

A look of horror came over Jeremy's face when he heard the mention of his name. He plopped down in the chair and started mumbling under his breath in a flabbergasted tone, "Me? I have AIDS? It can't be."

WHAT'S THE MATTER, CASANOVA? DIDN'T YOU KNOW YOU HAD AIDS?

Jeremy felt like he had a huge lump stuck in his throat as he slowly shook his head. Then he heard the faint sound of a fipple flute playing the *Death March*. He stared off into space mumbling in a whisper, "How long do I have before I have to pay the piper?"

YOU DON'T WANT TO KNOW.

Tears welled up in his eyes as he thought about losing his life. He sniffled, "I don't want to die. I'm afraid."

YOU SHOULD HAVE THOUGHT ABOUT THAT BEFORE YOU CLIMBED INTO BED WITH ALL THOSE PROMISCUOUS WOMEN.

Jeremy got up out of the chair and wiped away his tears. He walked over to the far corner of the room feeling like nothing mattered anymore. He didn't know what else to do so he just peered into the dark cells. Seeing one empty, he said haughtily, "I don't hear any misery coming out of this cell. What happened? Did Baal-ze...bug slip up and let one fly away?"

IF YOU MUST KNOW, I'M HOLDING CELL 666 FOR DESTINY.

All of a sudden, the door opened to expose two warlocks standing outside.

GO WITH THEM. THEY WILL TAKE YOU BACK TO THE MANSION.

As Jeremy walked out the door feeling extremely depressed, the ghostly clone vanished.

IF I WERE YOU JEREMY, I'D LIVE IT UP WHILE I STILL CAN.

12

Melissa was sitting at the table sipping a glass of ice water when Charles walked into the diner carrying an empty jar. She motioned to her brother and he sat down at the table across from her.

"I already ordered," said Melissa.

The waitress hurried over to the table and poured Charles a glass of ice water.

When she offered him a menu, he said, "Betty, I'll just have the usual."

"Yes sir," she replied in her southern accent and then walked away.

When Charles set the glass container down on the table, Melissa turned up her slightly pug nose in disgust and said, "No way."

Gently tapping on the wall beside her, she queried, "Cockroaches, right? I knew it."

Charles laughed and said, "No."

"Then why the bug jar?"

He leaned across the table, keeping his voice low so no one else could hear him. "Remember the stink bug I put in here?"

She peered into the jar and said in a hushed tone, "Yeah, so, where is it?"

He shrugged and said, "I don't know. It disappeared."

"I thought you put a lid on it."

"I did but somehow it got out."

She raised her voice upsettingly, "You mean that little stinker's running around the classroom somewhere?"

Charles motioned for Melissa to lower her voice. "Would you keep a lid on it?"

She whispered back snootily, "Fine, but don't expect me to come to class until you find that thing."

He smiled at her and said, "Hey, speaking of class, what time's church on Sunday?"

She grinned from ear to ear and replied, "Ten o'clock, same time as usual, why?"

He leaned back against the seat with his hands clasped behind his head. "I've been thinking about going back to church."

"Uh-huh," she uttered suspiciously.

Betty returned and set two cokes and two straws down on the table.

"Thank you, Betty," Charles said politely.

"You're welcome," replied Betty and then headed towards the kitchen.

"This doesn't have anything to do with Destiny, does it?" inquired Melissa.

"I can't seem to get her out of my mind."

"Yeah right, you and about a hundred other guys; not to change the subject, but are you going to help Jeremy?"

"He's beyond help. Besides, I tried sharing Jesus with him again before he took that stupid trip to Egypt, and all he did was laugh at me."

"So what if he laughed at you. You've got to keep trying to save him. As long as there is breath left in his body, you go right on speaking the Word of God to him. You and I both know the only one who can save Jeremy from drowning in hell is Jesus. Please, Charles, don't turn your back on him."

"If Jeremy wants to fritter away his life and die before his time, that's his business."

Melissa frowned at her brother and said, "What happened to you, Charles? You used to give the shirt off your back if you thought it would help somebody."

Charles crossed his arms and pursed his lips, full of pride. "Well maybe I've had one too many times at bat, and now it's my turn to sit the bench."

"Have you forgotten about the time you got really drunk and almost drowned in the lake? Jeremy didn't hesitate for a second to try and save you."

As Charles mused over the past, he recalled almost every detail of that night.

It was a time when he and Jeremy were only nineteen years old, footloose and fancy-free, without a care in the world. They were attending a prestigious university in New York City and didn't give much thought to anything except studying, chasing girls, and partying on weekends.

One Saturday night, during one of the coldest months of the year, they took a small boat out on to the lake and started drinking. Charles got really drunk and threw the oars into the water.

"What did you do that for?" Jeremy shouted with irritation in his voice.

Then he flew to the edge of the boat to retrieve the paddles before they drifted away. When he discovered they were too far out of reach, he complained bitterly, "Oh great, now how are we supposed to get back to the dock?"

Charles didn't seem to care about their precarious predicament. He just climbed up on the front of the boat and continued acting like a child.

Jeremy scolded him firmly, "Charles, get down from there, you might fall! And give me that bottle of scotch. I should have never encouraged you to drink. You can't hold your liquor, buddy."

Charles responded with slurred speech, "Oh come on, Jeremys, don't be such a party poopser, heeheehee."

"Charles, be careful. You almost fell."

Charles flapped his arms up and down like a bird in flight and chuckled, "I'm not goings to fall. I knows what I be doing. See, I can fwy. I got wings."

"You don't have wings, Charles. Now get down from there before the wind pushes you off the boat."

"No!" Charles said defiantly.

"All right, that's it. I've had it. I'll get you down myself."

The moment Jeremy moved toward his inebriated friend, Charles chuckled mischievously and took a rebellious step backwards. As a result of his playful behavior, he lost his footing and plunged into the icy water—screaming bloody murder. He was only in the cold water for a moment before his jaw starting shivering so hard he could hardly speak. "Jer-Jer-Jere-my, hel-hel-help me pl-please. The wa-water is so-so-so co-cold."

Poor Charles, he seemed to have sobered up real quick.

Jeremy shouted, "Hang on, buddy, I'll throw you a life jacket."

Jeremy searched frantically for a vest among the other items in the boat, but when he couldn't find one, he cried out worriedly, "Charles, what did you do with our life jackets?"

Charles answered fretfully, "I uh mus-must have lef-left them on-on the dock."

Despair immediately struck a chord in Jeremy's soul as he looked towards the dock and saw the vests lying there. He shut his eyes tightly and groaned within himself, "Oh no."

Jeremy tried not to go to pieces as he thought about what he was going to do next. Then he got down on his knees and extended his arm out to Charles. "Here, Charles, grab my hand. We've got to get you out of that cold water before you get hypothermia. Your skin's turning purple."

"I ca-can't re-reach you. I'm too-too far a-away fro-from the bo-boat."

Jeremy shouted in a voice of desperation, "Come on, Charles, you got to try! Now swim to me."

Charles spluttered, "I can't. The current is pull-pulling me-me un-under. Ple-please, Jer-Jer-Jeremy, I'm so-so scare-scared."

The very next moment, Charles disappeared under the water. Instantly, a look of horror swept over Jeremy's face as he waited patiently for his friend to resurface from the cold murky water. When he didn't come up right away, Jeremy panicked and started screaming out his name, "Charles! Charles!"

The wind was now blowing so hard it was tossing the boat to and fro, shoving it further and further away from the dock.

All at once, Charles resurfaced spitting water out of his mouth. He was so cold he could hardly breathe. He gasped and then choked on water that had forced its way down his throat. He cried out in a fluster with shivering lips, "Jer-Je-Jeremy, I-I got-got a cra-cramp in my-my le-leg. I ca-can't fe-feel my-my le-legs any mo-more."

Suddenly, he disappeared underneath the water.

Jeremy knew it was suicide to jump into the freezing water, but he couldn't bare the thought of losing his best friend. He boldly cried out, "Don't worry, Charles, I got your back, buddy."

Then he dove into the water.

That night, Jeremy couldn't explain how he was able to handle the cold water long enough to rescue his friend. The strong current he had to swim against seemed impossible. Somehow, he managed to get Charles back into the boat and then gave him mouth to mouth resuscitation until he started breathing on his own. He also remembered stripping his wet clothes off and wrapping his cold body in warm blankets he had stowed in the boat. But everything after that was a blur until he and Charles woke up in the emergency room. How they got there he didn't know. It was nothing short of a miracle.

Charles looked over at Melissa as if waking up from a dream. "Yeah, he was always looking out for me. Did you know we both made a vow that night to never drink again? And to this day, neither one of us has. I'm surprised Jeremy told you about that."

He sighed heavily and said, "Melissa, I love Jeremy. I'm just sick and tired of being the blunt end of his jokes every time I talk about Jesus."

"Charles, if we don't forgive others, how can we say the love of Jesus Christ is in our hearts? So what if he laughed at you a few times, big deal. The important thing is you planted the right seed into Jeremy's heart by speaking God's words."

"You really think so?"

"Yeah, and I'm sure Jeremy's thought about those words, oh I'd say at least a dozen times."

Betty returned to the table carrying two lunch plates. "Here you go, one soup and sandwich and a burger and fries for the lady."

After Betty put the plate down in front of Melissa, Melissa immediately lifted the lid of the bun to check her burger.

"Is something wrong?" asked Betty.

Melissa's eyes widened with embarrassment as she slowly looked up at Betty. She didn't know the waitress had been watching her. "Wrong? Uh…no; I was just checking to make sure nothing crawled in with my burger."

Charles kicked Melissa under the table.

"Ouch! I mean that it was plain."

Betty didn't understand what Melissa was talking about so she just looked at her funny. "Can I get you anything else?"

Charles promptly replied, "No thank you, Betty. That will be all."

"Okay, enjoy your meal," said Betty.

Charles picked up his soup spoon and saw a message floating on top of his alphabet soup that read, *HELP JEREMY*. Instantly, his mouth dropped open in shock.

When Melissa saw her brother's eyes filled with anxiety, she queried concernedly, "Charles, what's the matter?"

Charles was too busy feeling convicted by the words he read and didn't answer.

"Charles, what's wrong?" she inquired persistently.

When her brother started taking off his shirt, Melissa fretfully looked about the diner to see if anybody was watching. She whispered to Charles in a high-pitched tone, "What are you doing?"

Charles handed Melissa his shirt and said, "I changed my mind. Give this to Jeremy."

She smiled warmly and said, "You bet I will; bro."

13

Worship music filled the main sanctuary in the Liberty Church while Pastor Sumner and his congregation of seven hundred people adored the Lord together.

Destiny was standing in the front row praying when she heard the voice of God say, "Seer, speak for me."

She nodded and then quickly found the scripture in her *Holy Bible* that God wanted her to share.

After the music stopped playing, the ebony-skinned Pastor picked up a microphone and told everyone to be seated. The entire congregation sat down with the exception of Destiny.

Pastor Sumner quickly acknowledged her presence by speaking to her in his African accent. "Destiny, do you have a word from the Lord?"

"Yes sir," she immediately replied.

Destiny carried her Bible up to the altar, and the Pastor handed her the microphone.

The young Prophetess looked about the congregation and boldly declared, "God wanted me to tell you, 'In the last days, false seers will come and deceive a lot of people. Many will turn away from God to betray and hate each other.'"

The Australian beauty held up the *Holy Bible* in her hand and continued uttering, "Dearly loved, we can't be participants with evil spirits and with God. Are we trying to provoke the Lord's jealousy? All images other than God's must vanish from our heart."

Destiny handed the microphone back to the Preacher and sat down.

Pastor Sumner smiled warmly at the prophetess and said, "Thank you, Destiny, for that word from the Lord."

Charles leaned over to Melissa and whispered, "Mercy! How do you get that to vanish from your heart?"

Melissa elbowed Charles and gave him a stern look. She was very disappointed that he was easily distracted from hearing the voice of God.

"What?" Charles whispered indignantly.

"Would you keep your mind on God?" she sternly whispered back.

Feeling prideful, Charles crossed his arms and began to pout.

The Pastor picked up his opened Bible from the podium and said, "Church, please open your Bibles to *Second Kings, Chapter One*."

The congregation quickly opened their Bibles and started thumbing through the pages to find the right book.

Charles couldn't see Destiny from where he was sitting so he scooted over in the pew.

The Preacher looked fondly around the room at the people attending worship and said, "In this chapter, we read about a man named Ahaziah who had an accident and wanted to know if he would recover. Unfortunately, Ahaziah was destined for ruin once he sought his future from Baal-zebub, which in Hebrew means *"lord of the fly,"* instead of the one true God."

Pastor Sumner glanced over at one of the servers in the audio booth and made a gesture with his hand. "Tom, can you run the videotape please?"

All of a sudden, a cartoon animation appeared on the projector screen showing a huge pot-bellied idol with a hideous-looking face hewn out of stone. As the idol mouthed its name, a swarm of flies spewed out of its mouth and quickly formed into the word: BAAL-ZEBUB.

Melissa and Charles exchanged a look of surprise and simultaneously whispered, "Jeremy."

The Minister went on to say, "It is said that Baal-zebub prophesied by the buzzing of flies. Since flies are nasty little pests that steal our time by getting us to chase after them, let's picture them in this cartoon illustration as evil seducing spirits."

To the surprise of the worshippers, the next cartoon that appeared on the screen was the Pastor. He was sitting in his rocking chair with an opened Bible in his lap, swatting at three pesky bee flies circling above his head. A giant screen television was directly in front of him with the word, BAAL-ZEBUB, spelled out across the screen with bodies of bee flies.

Pastor Sumner pointed to the flies on the screen and said, "Seducing spirits try to steal our time with God by luring us into idol worship. The devil knows if he can get us to fill our belly with idolatrous thoughts, we'll stop speaking about God. For example, if he can get us to make sports our God, we'll talk about sports all the time. If it's money, we'll talk about money all the time. If it's idle talk, we can't wait until we share all the latest juicy gossip. If it's worry, we'll talk about our problems all the time. It all starts with a buzzing in the ear."

To get his point across in a more dramatic way, the Preacher quickly altered his voice to imitate a fly. "Buzz, Buzz, Buzz, Pastor, wouldn't you rather be watching television than reading that boring Bible?"

The congregation laughed loudly at the Minister's comical portrayal of a fly's voice.

"Remember, an idol is anything we chase after more than God," the Pastor added.

After pointing to the word, BAAL-ZEBUB, on the projector screen, the Preacher explained, "The word "BAAL" means, *lord or master*. So whatever consumes our thoughts more than

God has become our Baal. Like I said before, for some of us it could be our television, sports, or money; for others, it could be movie stars, food, fame, alcohol, drugs, gambling, video games, gossip, sex, worry, or even work. God warned us that in the last days, people would become lovers of themselves instead of lovers of Him. Beloved, we don't want to be like the world."

The congregation chuckled when they saw the cartoon television turn into a pile of dung. Then the three flies that were pestering the minister flew over and sat on top of the manure. The caricature of the pastor continued rocking in his chair, still reading the *Holy Bible* with a big grin on his face.

Pastor Sumner pointed to the dung in the illustration and said animatedly, "Seducing spirits are drawn to idol worship like flies on—I think you get the picture. The only way to get rid of these seducing spirits is to remove the dung or the Baal from our heart. I ask everyone here to learn from Ahaziah's mistake. Don't turn your heart into a deathbed by giving it to another god. It's time we tell Baal-zebub to buzz off. God's place must be number one not number two."

The congregation clapped and cheered loudly as one man shouted, "Good word, Pastor!"

Pastor Sumner closed the service with prayer and the congregation disbanded.

Directly afterward, Jeremy walked into the back of the church rubbing his hands together. He lustfully eyed all the beautiful women strolling by and then whispered to the evil spirit within him, "Okay, which one is she?"

SHE'S THE ELDER STANDING IN FRONT OF THE ALTAR PRAYING OVER THE BALD MAN. HER NAME IS JANET.

The Professor looked toward the altar and saw a woman in her early forties praying over a heavyset bald man. He crinkled up his nose in repulsion and nosily objected, "No way! I'm not sleeping with her. She's ugly."

A couple passing by overheard Jeremy and looked at him strangely.

After nervously clearing his throat, the Professor cunningly remarked, "Uh...the Pastor's right, evil is ugly. You don't want to sleep with it."

The couple nodded their head in agreement and walked on.

Jeremy rolled his eyes and let out a big breath. "Whew! That was close."

Staring back at the elder, Jeremy whispered belligerently to the evil voice inside him, "There is no way I'm sleeping with her. I'm leaving."

All of a sudden, Jeremy felt terrible stabbing pains rippling through his abdomen. Right away, he clutched his tummy and doubled over groaning, "Ooooooh!"

The Professor tried to conceal his discomfort so he wouldn't draw attention to himself and then finally threw in the towel. "All right, all right, I'll do it. Just stop the pain, please."

Instantly, the pain subsided. After the bald man walked away, Jeremy nonchalantly sauntered over to Elder Janet.

"Would you like prayer?" inquired Janet as he walked up.

Jeremy stared passionately into her eyes and said conceitedly, "I'm the answer to your prayers."

"What?"

"You've been praying for a husband right?"

"How did you know that? I never told anyone."

He grinned from ear to ear and replied shrewdly, "You told God."

Janet smiled after hearing his reply.

Jeremy held out his hand and said, "Let me formally introduce myself, I'm Professor Jeremy Thompson."

She shook his hand and queried, "A professor, huh? What field of study?"

"Entomology."

"So you're a bug lover."

"Yes. I'm especially fond of the dragonfly. I love to watch its crafty mind capture unsuspecting flies and devour them."

Janet cleared her throat feeling uncomfortable by the way he was looking at her. He spoke as if she was the unsuspecting fly he was about to devour.

Jeremy glanced over at Destiny talking to the Pastor and immediately changed the subject. "Listen, Janet, I was wondering, would you like to go out with me?"

Completely stunned by his offer, she asked, "You are a very attractive man. Why would you want to go out with me?"

With a devilish smirk on his face, he replied deceitfully, "Because you're my destiny."

The heart of Elder Janet was wooed by his crafty words. She smiled and replied enthusiastically, "That's so sweet. Yes. I'd love to go out with you."

"How about dinner at the Chateau Friday night?"

"The Chateau? Are you sure you want to go there? That's the most expensive place in town."

"You let me worry about that. Is it a date?"

She smiled full of excitement and answered back, "Why not."

"Great. I'll pick you up outside the Church at six-thirty."

"Okay."

As Jeremy walked away, Janet sensed something wasn't quite right about this man. She felt alarms going off inside her, but allowed her desperation for a husband to override her better judgment. After all, she wasn't getting any younger. She wanted children of her own and knew her biological clock was ticking.

Jeremy was on his way out of the church when he spotted Charles and Melissa heading towards the altar to see Destiny. He thought aloud, "Hey, it's Charles. I better go over and say hello."

The Professor hurried toward the altar until he again felt intense pain in his stomach. He clutched his belly and doubled over moaning, "Oh, that hurts!"

Then he heard Baal-zebub's evil thoughts buzzing inside his mind.

YOU'D LIKE ME A WHOLE LOT MORE IF YOU'D QUIT RESISTING ME. I SAID STAY AWAY FROM DESTINY. I DON'T WANT TO RISK BEING SEEN BEFORE I GET THE CHANCE TO GET EVEN WITH HER.

Jeremy whined bitterly, "I wasn't doing anything wrong. I was just going to see an old friend of mine."

IF YOU ARE REFERRING TO CHARLES, HE'S NOT YOUR FRIEND. HE BETRAYED YOU BY TELLING SWEET INNOCENT MELISSA THAT YOU'RE A SCHIZOPHRENIC. NOW SHE THINKS YOU'RE A FREAK. IF I WERE YOU, I'D GET EVEN WITH HIM.

Jeremy shook his head refusing to believe the accusations against Charles that were drumming inside his head. He loved his friend like a brother and didn't want to believe he would ever betray him.

YOU DON'T HAVE TO TAKE MY WORD FOR IT. CALL MELISSA UP AND ASK HER.

As the Professor mediated on Baal-zebub's evil thoughts, his countenance changed to a look of hate. He sneered at Charles like he was his worst enemy and stormed out of the building.

14

Charles kissed Melissa on the side of the head and said in a hushed tone, "All right, little sister, I think I can take it from here."

Melissa just stood there staring at her brother so he whispered a little louder in her ear. "Disappear!"

"Fine, but you're wasting your time lover-boy."

As Melissa walked away, he said grumpily, "Would you quit calling me that?"

Charles strolled over to Destiny who was busy arranging flowers in a huge crystal vase. Trying to be inconspicuous, he slowly crept up behind her. Sensing his presence, she quickly turned around. Shocked to see her teacher standing there, she nervously blurted out, "Professor, I…I didn't know you attended Liberty."

Once again, Charles found himself at a loss for words as he stood there facing Destiny."

"Professor…Professor?"

As if awakening from a deep sleep, he slowly answered, "Please…call me Charles."

She smiled at him warmly and said, "How long have you been attending Liberty?"

When the googol-eyed professor failed to answer her, she gently touched him on the shoulder and asked concernedly, "Professor, are you all right?"

Aroused by her touch and the smell of her perfume, his eyes instantly rolled up in his head, and he pushed her hand away. "Please, don't do that!"

Feeling extremely embarrassed by his reaction, her face turned beet red. She whispered shakily under her breath, "Sorry."

Destiny immediately turned around and continued arranging the flowers.

Charles stared blankly at the back of her head not knowing what to say. He reached down and picked up some of the flowers off the platform. "Here, let me help you."

Destiny stood quietly watching him put the flowers in the vase and then sniffed the red rose in her hand. To break the ice, she said passionately, "I love flowers. They remind me of the heart."

"How's that?"

She gently stroked one of the petals on the rose and replied caringly, "They're so delicate you have to be careful how you touch them."

Charles continued to be enthralled as he listened to her talk. "You're accent is beautiful, Australian, right?"

She nodded.

"So how did you wind up in New Orleans?"

"My mother grew up here. She decided to move back to Louisiana after my dad died a couple years ago."

"I'm sorry. I know what it's like to lose someone you love. Our parents were killed in an automobile accident when Melissa was only twelve. Believe me, raising her hasn't been easy."

Destiny smiled and said, "So who stole your southern accent?"

"Never had one, I'm Jewish. At least half of me is...I mean am. Melissa and I are from New York City, same as Jeremy. We've only been living in New Orleans for about seven years.

They had cutbacks at my old job so Jeremy helped me get a job down here. He took a position at the University here right after he graduated from college. So tell me something, Destiny, why did you take my class? You don't seem particularly interested in Entomology?"

"I picked it as an elective. It was either that or—ugh—Psychology 101."

Charles replied disappointingly, "Oh. So what's your major?"

"Creative Arts," she said happily.

"Any particular field you like the most?"

Destiny's eyes sparkled as she thought about her passions work. "I love ballet, drama, classical music, and writing Christian novels."

"So you're a writer, huh?"

She nodded agreeably.

"I see we have something in common. I love to write too. In fact, I teach a class on creative writing at the college. Maybe you'd like to take it some time."

She accidentally dropped the rose on the ground and said, "I don't think so. I've already taken several courses on creative writing already."

Feeling rejected, he responded gloomily, "Oh."

Charles bent down to pick up the flower she dropped and subsequently handed it back to her. "Destiny, would you be interested in helping me and my sister find Jeremy?"

"Sure, I'd be glad to help. I've been praying for Jeremy ever since the day Melissa told me about him."

Melissa snuck up behind her brother to eavesdrop on his conversation.

"Uh…Destiny, would you…um…would you like to get something to eat?" Charles asked nervously.

Destiny gazed into his beautiful big green eyes and then shyly looked away. "No thank you. I'm having lunch with my mother."

She quickly put the rose into the vase and stepped down from the altar.

Charles suddenly felt unsure of himself as he watched Destiny flee from his presence.

Melissa tapped her brother on the shoulder to get his attention. Then she snickered playfully while pretending to swing a bat. "Strike one!"

He replied annoyingly to her ill-timed gesture. "Very funny, I think you've been playing too much softball lately, sis. Maybe we should find you a new hobby."

15

Jeremy held the passenger door open while Janet climbed into a very expensive sports car.

After driving a mile down the road, it started pouring rain. Jeremy turned on the windshield wipers and said, "I hope you don't mind, but I took the liberty of changing our plans for tonight. I thought it might be more romantic if we had a quiet candlelight dinner for two at my place."

Janet's eyes widened with worry as she resounded, "At your place?"

"Is something wrong?"

"No," she nervously replied.

Jeremy turned on the radio and queried, "What would you like to listen to?"

Janet took a quick peek at her makeup in the rearview mirror and answered cheerily, "How about the Christian channel?"

The Professor puckered his lips as if he'd just eaten something sour. "Sorry, I never get that channel."

Jeremy pushed one of the buttons on the radio and a man's voice came on singing, "Love is just a fling, it doesn't mean a thing."

"How about this one?" he said with a mischievous grin.

Janet quickly shut off the radio and replied offensively, "Ugh! That's disgusting."

"What did you do that for?" he growled angrily.

"I don't want to listen to someone singing about things I don't believe in."

"It's just a stupid song. It doesn't mean anything."
"Then why listen to it?"
"Because I like the beat."
Janet shook her head in disgust. "Oh please. If you allow evil words to fill your heart, eventually they're going to overflow out of your mouth."

Jeremy made an ugly face at Janet while she was busy brushing her hair and then started singing the song again out of spite. "Love is just a fling. It doesn't mean a thing."

"What do you think you're doing?" she inquired in an aggravated tone.

He snickered impishly under his breath. "Oh, sorry, I guess you're right. The words do come out of you."

Janet felt the tension mounting between her and Jeremy while she sat quietly listening to the windshield wipers scraping back and forth on the glass.

About a half hour later, Jeremy pulled into the driveway of a huge mansion.

"This is where you live?" she asked shockingly.

"Yeah."

"How can you afford all this on a professor's pay?"

"Uh...my father left me a lot of money when he died," he retorted deceitfully.

"Oh."

Jeremy got out of the car and opened the door for Janet. He said impatiently, "Come on, we better hurry inside before it starts raining again. I don't want my hair to get messed up."

After he slammed the car door, they made haste for the mansion and subsequently went inside.

While putting her coat and purse in the hall closet, Jeremy eyed himself in the mirror on the other side of the door. After quickly raising his eyebrows several times out of vain conceit, he discreetly blew himself a kiss. Then he closed the door and said, "I gave the staff the night off just so we could be alone."

Janet began fidgeting nervously as she looked around the room. She didn't know how she was going to hide the fact that she was very uncomfortable to be alone with a man she hardly even knew.

Jeremy took Janet by the arm and said, "Right this way my lady. Allow me to escort you into the formal dinning area."

The moment Janet stepped into the room she was in awe at the beautiful décor. "That's a beautiful crystal chandelier you have hanging above the dining table. And these oil paintings on the wall are absolutely gorgeous. They must have cost you a fortune. I'm impressed. Everything looks so beautiful."

With guile in his tongue, he replied, "That's only because you're here."

Embarrassed by his flattering remark, Janet's face flushed red.

Jeremy pulled out a chair under the dining table. Once she was seated, he opened a box of matches and lit the wick on the black candlestick. He blew out the match and queried, "How about some wine?"

"Sure, I'd love some."

Jeremy smirked roguishly while slowly pouring the wine into her glass. His sagacious mind thought his plan was working perfectly. Janet was falling right into his trap.

The clever fox raised his glass into the air with a hint of trickery in his eyes and said, "A toast to your beauty."

She immediately started blushing again and turned away, replying awkwardly, "Jeremy, I don't know what to say."

The Professor snickered under his breath while her head was turned, "Lady, get real, have you looked in the mirror lately?"

Jeremy touched her hand to get her attention and said insistently, "Come on, drink up."

"Okay," she giggled and then gulped down the wine.

When she burped loudly, Jeremy rolled his eyes in abhorrence and thought, *What a pig!*

She instantly cupped her hand over her mouth as another gas bubble escaped through her nose. "Oh, excuse me. I'm so sorry, how embarrassing."

When Jeremy tried to pour Janet more wine, she quickly put her hand over the top of the glass and said, "No, I better not. I don't want to get drunk."

"Janet, do you actually think I'd let that happen? This isn't some cheap wine like you're used to drinking. You'd have to consume at least six glasses before you could get a buzz off this stuff."

"Really?"

Jeremy pulled her hand away and refilled the glass. "Would I lie to you?"

Suddenly, three bee flies appeared buzzing around Janet's head as she emptied her glass for the second time.

The Professor checked the time on his watch and said, "The caterers don't get here until eight so why don't we go sit by the fireplace?"

Jeremy grabbed Janet by the hand and pulled her into the living room. Then he sat down on the couch and patted the cushion next to him. "Janet, sit beside me."

Janet felt very uneasy about sitting that close to him so she walked across the room to admire the dancing flames in the fireplace. "That's the biggest fireplace I've ever seen."

"Come on, Janet, sit beside me," he requested persistently.

She continued to ignore him as she warmed herself by the fire. "Jeremy, explain something to me. If you gave the staff the night off, who started the fire?"

"Oh...uh...it's run by an automatic timer."

"Oh."

He grinned wickedly and said, "Come on, Janet, sit down. Don't be afraid. You can trust me. Why I wouldn't hurt a fly."

While Jeremy was chuckling under his breath, the ghostly Dragonfly materialized within the flames and growled abhorrently at the unsuspecting Elder. It was a good thing she couldn't see the beast or it might have scared her half to death.

Once more, Jeremy patted the seat. "Janet, sit next to me. I promise you, I don't bite."

A faint smile crossed Janet's homely face, and she heaved a sigh of concession. "Okay."

16

Little did Jeremy know "*The Seer*" was sitting in her living room praying to God on his behalf, "Lord Jesus, I know this lady's always bugging you about something, but I really need to find Jeremy. I know you're drawing him to you by the power of your Holy Spirit, and I want to help by telling him that you love him.

Feeling extremely tired, Destiny laid her head back against the maroon-colored, Queen Victorian style chair. Suddenly, she saw a vision of herself giggling as a ladybug landed on her right index finger. The Australian beauty laughed knowing what the ladybug represented until she heard a woman's voice screaming in the distance. As Destiny slowly turned around to see where the voice was coming from, the ladybug flew away.

Peering into a dark place, she saw a man's hand pouring a potion into Janet's wine glass. Horrified by what she saw, she cried out in tears, "No!"

Immediately, Destiny was filled with boldness by the power of the Holy Spirit and shouted, "In the mighty name of Jesus, I command you evil spirit to get your hands off her. Janet, don't drink the wine!"

After the vision ended, Destiny opened her eyes and smiled. She knew God had prompted her to pray for Janet and that everything would be okay.

17

Meanwhile on the other side of town, Jeremy was pouring Janet another glass of wine.

The moment her back was turned, the nutty Professor took a tube of hallucinogenic out of his suit pocket and poured it into her glass. He carefully stirred the potion into the wine with his index finger and then set her glass down on the coffee table next to his.

Soon as Janet turned back around, Jeremy took her into his arms and said ardently, "You are so beautiful."

The Professor gently touched her trembling lips and started passionately kissing her. After several moments of heavy breathing, she pulled away from him and declared distressingly, "I can't do this!"

He gazed erotically into her eyes and whispered innocently, "Janet, don't you desire me?"

Tears filled her eyes as she fervently replied, "Oh yes. But I know in order to do this I'd have to turn against my God….and I love him more than that."

The immoral spirit within Jeremy wickedly advised, "Come on, Janet. You don't have anything to worry about. You have God's grace. He'll forgive you."

When Jeremy tried to kiss her again, she immediately pushed him away, protesting loudly, "No!"

Janet quickly stood to her feet and stated adamantly, "This was a mistake. I got to go."

"Janet, please don't go. I promise I won't. Please stay."

She laid her hand on the side of his handsome face and said, "All right, I'll stay, but only for a few more minutes."

Jeremy picked up the two wine glasses off the table and handed the Mickey Finn to Janet. The sly fox grinned naughtily and said, "A toast to our eternal friendship."

"To our eternal friendship," she resounded.

Just as Janet was about to take a sip of wine, she heard Destiny's voice calling out to her. "Janet, don't drink the wine!"

"What?" she gasped fearfully and then slowly looked around the room.

Jeremy touched her hand and queried, "Janet is something wrong?"

Startled by his touch, she shrieked and snatched her hand away.

"What's the matter with you?"

The extremely jittery Elder didn't answer him. She set her glass down on the table and fled the room.

"Janet! Janet, come back here!" he shouted frustratingly while chasing after her.

Janet completely ignored his request and quickly grabbed her coat and purse out of the hall closet. Then she took her cell phone out of her purse and dialed for a cab.

"Where are you going?"

Janet opened the front door and replied firmly, "Home; I know I've had too much to drink when I hear Destiny calling."

He puckered his brow and queried, "What is that supposed to mean?"

She gave him a quick peck on the cheek and whispered, "I'll see you later."

"No, let me give you a ride," he uttered back pushily.

Janet shook her head and closed the door behind her.

Enraged by her sudden departure, Jeremy stammered into the living room and glared at the ghostly Dragonfly within the flames. Having to admit defeat, they both simultaneously screamed in a fit of rage, "Destiny!"

18

Charles and Melissa stood quietly outside the door of the huge mansion. It was Saturday around noon when Charles rang the doorbell.

"Charles, are you sure this is the right address?"

Losing patience after she asked him the same question three times, Charles mockingly retorted, "Yes, I'm sure this is the right address."

He took a piece of cardboard out of his wallet and handed it to Melissa. "I tore this off the box Jeremy sent me. See, it says, 666 Backwords Drive. It's the same address I gave to Destiny after class yesterday."

"But how can Jeremy afford a place like this? And did you see that car parked in the driveway with his name on the license plate? Oh man, it is so tight."

Charles shrugged and said, "I don't know, maybe he applied and got welfare or something."

As he thought about what he just said, he chuckled, "I crack myself up."

Melissa giggled at her brother's wisecrack and then punched him teasingly on the arm. "You're cracked up all right. I just wish I could find all the pieces so I can put you back together."

Charles stuck his tongue out at her and snickered under his breath. Then he rang the doorbell again. When nobody answered, he said, "I don't think anybody's home."

"There's got to be somebody here. Look at all the cars parked outside."

He sighed heavily and said, "All right, I'll try it again."

Melissa looked up and down the street. "I thought you said Destiny was coming?"

Charles checked his watch and said, "I guess she couldn't make it."

Melissa gazed admiringly at the beautiful bright blue sky. "Isn't it a gorgeous day? The sun is shining, and the birds are chirping."

"It sure is. With all the rain we've had lately, it's a nice change. Oh by the way, did you remember to fill up the car with gas after school?"

"I couldn't fill it up. You didn't give me enough money."

"I gave you forty dollars."

"You know the price of gas has gone sky high ever since Charter Road gave that prophetic word to the church."

"What word?"

"Oh, I forgot. You haven't been to church in awhile. Anyway, she prayed to God about the gas prices, and He gave her a prophetic word."

"What did He say?"

"God's going to bring the gas prices down to a mere ten cents a gallon."

Doubting the prophetic word, Charles said, "That's impossible. The only way that can happen is if gasoline is no longer valuable because of overabundance, or it becomes obsolete in the future."

"I don't know about that, but I'm just glad God's going to help us. I think if we spent more time praying about things instead of complaining about them, a lot of things would change."

"You're absolutely right, sis. Thank you, Jesus, for bringing down those gas prices."

Melissa promptly joined her heart in agreement with the Word of God and said, "Amen!"

The very next moment, a car pulled up in the driveway. Charles excitedly proclaimed, "She's here!"

He hurried over and opened the car door for Destiny.

She climbed out of the car and said, "Sorry, I'm late. My mom needed me to run some errands for her."

"That's okay," said Charles as he walked her to the front door.

Destiny acknowledged Melissa's presence and then gave her a big hug. When the girls started to chitchat, Charles rudely interrupted them. "I rang the doorbell several times, but Jeremy didn't answer. Either he didn't hear me or he's not home. I'll ring it one more time just to make sure."

Charles rang the doorbell and a young witch answered the door. She inquired impolitely, "What do you want?"

The extreme nervousness in Charles' voice was evidenced when he answered stuttering, "I'm...uh...uh...."

Talking faster, he said, "I'm looking for a buddy of mine."

"And you think he's here?" the witch snapped annoyingly.

"Yes ma'am. His name's uh...."

Charles snapped his fingers several times and continued mumbling, "Uh...uh...."

Melissa rolled her eyes at her brother and then shook her head in exasperation. Trying to be humorous, she said to the witch, "Sorry, lady, my brother seems to have stepped on his tongue."

Destiny tried to hold in the laughter as she watched Charles desperately trying to spit out the right words.

Charles mumbled frustratingly, "I know what it is; it's right on the tip of my tongue. It's uh...uh...."

Bothered by his stupidity, the impatient witch crossed her arms and said sarcastically, "Well, don't hurt yourself."

Melissa finally blurted out, "His name is Jeremy Thompson, okay."

Charles' eyes lit up with recollection upon hearing his friend's name. "Oh yeah."

"You're friends with Jeremy?" queried the witch.

Charles nodded.

The witch responded with open arms. "Well, why didn't you say so? Come on in."

She quickly grabbed Charles by the arm and pulled him inside the mansion.

Melissa shrugged as she looked over at Destiny, and then they both followed Charles inside.

Grinning from ear to ear, the witch lustfully remarked, "Jeremy's such a cutie. He's sure got a way with women."

Charles rolled his eyes and grumbled under his breath, "Oh brother."

"Yep, that sounds like our Jeremy, all right," said Melissa.

"Right this way," uttered the witch.

The young woman dressed in all black escorted the guests down a hallway and then behind some huge black curtains. "You'll have to wait back here until the meetings over. The high priest won't let you in without being properly dressed. Sorry I can't stay, but I have to join the others."

The witch quickly walked away.

Melissa brushed her bangs out of her eyes and queried, "High priest? What is she talking about?"

"I don't know," replied Charles.

Charles cracked the curtains and peeked into a huge ballroom filled with over two hundred people. After eyeballing everyone in the room, he said in a barely audible voice, "I don't see what's his name."

"Me either," whispered Melissa.

Charles noticed all the people were wearing black. "So who died?"

Melissa shrugged her shoulders.

Destiny cut in on their conversation, answering quietly, "It's a coven."

Charles immediately retorted, "Ugh!"

Melissa spoke just above a whisper, "You mean this is one of Satan's churches?"

Destiny nodded.

"Sick! Why would anyone want to worship something dead?"

Charles shrugged as he watched a demonically-influenced middle-aged man walk to the front of the congregation.

The warlock picked up the microphone and said loudly, "May I have your attention, please?"

The coven quieted down so that you could hear a pin drop.

Charles spoke softly to Destiny, "Who's that guy supposed to be?"

Destiny replied in a whisper, "I think he's the high priest she was talking about."

"Oh."

The warlock continued speaking, "Beelzebub is planning another attack against the Liberty Church. This time, Satan promises 'The gates of hell will prevail!'"

The cult cheered and applauded at their dark lord's boisterous declaration.

Charles scoffed under his breath, "You idiot! God said, 'The gates of hell will not prevail against His church!'"

Shaking his head in disgust, he added, "Talk about the blind leading the blind."

Destiny eyed the huge black diamond ring on the man's left index finger. Then she recalled the beautiful white diamond ring God had shown her. The Australian beauty stared at the satanic priest while whispering under her breath, "The poor thing is *Stone* blind."

"*Stone* blind? What do you mean?" asked Charles.

"Satan has deceived all these people into thinking his voice is something to be treasured, but we all know the real gem is Jesus Christ."

"Amen!"

"Listen up! I want everyone to get into their prayer circles," the high priest commanded.

Without hesitation, the coven members grabbed each other's hands and formed into groups of six.

Charles frowned instantly at the high priest when he started leading the coven in demonic chanting, "Death, death, death!"

Melissa whispered to Destiny, "What are they doing?"

"I believe they're trying to cast a spell on our church in Beelzebub's name."

"Oh give me a break. Don't they know Satan can't spell? If he could, he'd know he can't curse what God has called blessed."

Charles replied, "Yeah, you'd think they'd wake up and have a clue by now. Year after year they curse the church, and year after year it keeps growing."

"I don't know about you guys, but I'm sick of all the *misspelling*. I'll wait for you outside," Melissa murmured on her way out of the room.

Charles found it more difficult to keep his eyes off Destiny once he was left alone with her in the room.

"Professor, I wish you would quit staring at me," Destiny requested upsettingly.

Then she stormed out of the room and Charles chased after her. Grabbing her by the arm, he spun her around and looked deep into her eyes. He said sorrowfully, "Do you know how frustrating it is to look at the most beautiful flower you've ever seen in your life and not be able to touch it?"

Destiny jerked away from him and hurried outside.

Charles pursued Destiny until he got directly in front of her path. "Destiny, listen to me. I wanted to make sure that what I was feeling in my heart was right. So I asked God last night if you were the one He had chosen for me. He said, 'Yes.'"

"No! That's not true. He wouldn't say that," she hollered disturbingly and then pushed passed him to get to her car.

Charles glanced over at his sister who was leaning against the building with her arms crossed. Soon as she saw him looking at her she pretended to swing a bat. While holding up two fingers, she mouthed the words, "Strike two."

Charles frowned at Melissa's juvenile behavior until he heard Destiny driving away. He immediately whirled around and angrily protested her expedient departure by smacking himself on the forehead. "Aaaaaagh! Why won't you let me get close to you?"

Melissa felt sorry for her downcast brother. She walked over and put her hand on his shoulder. "If you're interested, bro, she told me she dances every Tuesday and Thursday night at seven."

"Where?" he eagerly inquired.

"At the Graceful Art Dance Studio."

19

Charles strolled into the Graceful Art Dance Studio feeling a bit uneasy. He didn't know how Destiny was going to react to him being there. As he thoroughly searched among the numerous male and female ballet dancers performing on the floor, he thought, *Where is she?*

He checked his watch and noticed the time was fifteen minutes past seven. Disappointed, he sighed heavily and then sat down in a chair. After squirming restlessly in his seat for another fifteen minutes, he decided to walk up to the desk clerk and ask where she was.

The desk clerk replied, "She's in a private room in the back. She's owns this studio."

"Oh. Thank you."

"You're welcome."

Charles slowly edged his way along the dimly lit hallway until he came to a huge room with mirrors covering the walls. Trying to keep a low profile, he took a quick peek around the corner. The moment he spotted Destiny, his mouth dropped open for she was a sight to behold. She was dressed in a beautiful, sparkling, baby blue leotard with a short flowing skirt.

As Charles stood there watching her dance the ballet, he was completely captivated by her beauty. He whispered ecstatically under his breath, "Oh, Destiny, how you make my soul dance."

After spying on her for several minutes, he decided to take his shoes off and go in and ask her to dance.

When Destiny saw him, she was taken aback and said disturbingly, "Charles, what are you doing here?"

He gently took her by the hand and stared avidly into her eyes.

She promptly rejected his touch by yanking her hand away and putting it behind her back. "Professor, please don't!"

Charles pleaded tenderly, "Destiny, dance with me, please."

She stared at him rigid for several moments without uttering a sound.

Offering his hand, he entreated, "Please."

When Destiny saw that Charles was unyielding she nervously placed her hand in his, and they both danced gracefully around the room.

Each time Charles held Destiny in his arms, her heart beat faster. She felt like a captive bird longing to fly away so she could be free of the passions stirring within her.

Sensing her emotions were hurtling out of control, she pulled away from Charles and hurried over to one of the stretching bars. While still trying to catch her breath, she slowly looked up and saw Charles staring intently at her reflection in the mirror.

His eyes stayed fixed on her as he spoke with great zeal. "All my life I've waited for you. You're the one I've prayed for…the mate for my soul."

Destiny eyes widened with uncertainty as she stared at Charles' reflection in the mirror. "No, that's not true."

Charles grabbed her by the arm and turned her towards him. He looked deep into her eyes as if he could see right through her and said, "You're trembling. You feel it too."

Raising her voice, she quickly rebuked him. "No!"

Charles placed his hands on the cheeks of her face and whispered, "Don't be afraid, Destiny, I won't hurt you."

He gently pressed his lips against hers, and she immediately pulled away from him.

After staring indifferently at her reflection in the mirror, Destiny lowered her head in shame.

Charles turned her towards him and peered lovingly into her unresponsive eyes. He said in a soft voice, "Destiny, let me love you."

He kissed her tenderly on her right temple, and she pushed him away crying, "I can't!"

Staring hypnotically at her face in the mirror, he whimpered, "No don't say that. Tell me that when I look into the mirror of your soul I'll find my reflection."

Tension mounted in her voice as she replied coldly, "No. I made a promise to God, and I intend to keep it. Now please leave."

Charles' eyes puddled with tears. "I can't let you go. You're my destiny. God promised me that I'm going to marry you, and I'll keep waiting as long as it takes."

"No! God wouldn't promise you that!"

"You know as well as I do, Destiny, that when you put your faith in God's Word, He'll move heaven and earth to fulfill it. You will be my bride."

She slowly shook her head in denial and replied sympathetically, "I'm sorry, Charles, you got the wrong Destiny."

Charles stared back at her reflection in the mirror and said frustratingly, "Why won't you let me get close to you?"

When she turned her back on him without uttering a word, he hung his head down and walked out of the room.

20

Jeremy strutted into the Liberty Church after the Sunday morning service as if he was the best thing that ever happened to the place. He looked around the main sanctuary and saw the congregation standing around talking. When he spotted Janet standing by the altar he hurried over and kissed her on the cheek. "Hi cutie!"

The Professor handed Janet a black rose he had hidden behind his back, and she looked at the flower offensively. Not wanting to hurt his feelings, she forced herself to crack a smile. "Thank you. It's uh…it's uh…it's a flower all right."

"Go on, smell it. It's scented with a beautiful fragrance."

Janet stared back at him with a blank look on her face thinking, *He must not know the black rose is a symbol of death, or he wouldn't have given me this nasty thing.*

"Go on, smell it."

She tried hard to fight a look of nausea while sniffing the wilted rose scented with primrose.

Jeremy scoped out the room and then spoke secretively in her ear. "Janet, can I talk to you about something?"

"Sure."

He led her by the hand into the far corner of the room to avoid being overheard. While pointing discreetly at Destiny, who was praying for a young woman at the altar, he spoke just above a whisper. "See that young blonde over there."

"Destiny?"

"Yeah, that floozy tried to seduce me."

Janet's eyes bulged with shock staring at the young prophetess. "What?"

Shaking her head vigorously, she said protectively, "No, that can't be. You must be mistaken. Destiny is sworn to celibacy. She would never do anything like that."

Jeremy snickered in a brash tone, "Celibacy? Oh please. I'm telling you that girl's loose as a goose."

The Professor had an evil grin on his face watching Janet stare dumbfounded at Destiny. He kissed the confused elder on the side of the cheek and said mischievously, "No offense, babe, but I'm sure glad I don't go to this church."

He chuckled mischievously under his breath and quickly walked away.

On his way out of the building, Jeremy overheard two warlocks from the coven in a heated dispute with Pastor Sumner.

"Frankly, Pastor, I'm appalled that you would allow this kind of a woman to be a leader in your church," one of the warlocks bitterly pointed out.

Pastor Sumner glanced back at Destiny with a look of bewilderment on his face. "Gentlemen, I don't know what to say. I can't believe it."

The other warlock snapped indignantly, "Well I do. We're not attending this church anymore. Good day, Pastor."

The Pastor just stood there completely stunned as the two warlocks and their wives stormed out of the building. Staring back at Destiny, he shook his head in exasperation and mumbled under his breath, "It can't be true. I know her spirit. She wouldn't do that."

The very next moment, Janet and Elder Ray, a bald-headed African-American in his early sixties, approached the Pastor and asked, "Pastor, can we speak to you privately for a moment?"

"Sure," the Pastor replied.

Then he escorted both Elders into a private room and shut the door behind him.

Several moments later, the Pastor opened the door and called out, "Destiny, come in here, please."

Destiny knew by the tone in the Pastor's voice that he was upset. She hurried over and asked suspiciously, "Is something wrong?"

The Pastor led her into the room and shut the door. He strongly requested, "Please sit down."

Destiny sat down with an uneasy feeling that she was about to be tried for a crime she didn't commit. She nervously shifted her eyes back and forth from the two Elders to the Pastor.

"Destiny, several men have accused you of trying to seduce them."

"What?" she repugnantly answered back.

Janet leaned over and whispered into the Minister's ear. "Pastor, her promiscuous lifestyle could explain why she's a bit clairvoyant."

Destiny overheard Janet and loudly protested, "Clairvoyant? How could you say that?"

The Pastor interrupted, "I'm sorry, Destiny, but I have no choice. Based upon the allegations against you, I have to take you out of leadership until a final determination can be made."

"But I haven't done anything wrong," she cried out in a pathetic whimper.

Elder Ray looked sorrowfully at Destiny, watching her fighting back the tears.

"It is also my recommendation that you seek private counsel with Elder Janet," the Pastor added.

Janet patted her hand and said, "We'll be praying for you, hon."

The distraught Prophetess pulled her hand away and quickly stood to her feet.

The Preacher firmly asserted, "Destiny, I warn you. If I have to, I will publicly excommunicate you in order to protect this church."

Destiny stared angrily at the Pastor and Elder Janet and then fled the room in tears.

Elder Ray promptly defended the young prophetess. "Pastor, I feel in my spirit that something's wrong. I beg you to reconsider your decision."

"These men are highly respected in this community. Why would they lie?" refuted Janet.

Elder Ray promptly contested, "Destiny's exposed evil coming against this church for almost two years now. Why would she suddenly turn against God?"

"That may be true, but you cannot deny the allegations against her," retorted Janet.

Pastor Sumner sighed heavily and nodded. "I agree with Elder Janet. My decision stands for now."

21

Destiny wandered through the forest of the woodlands with tears cascading down her cheeks. She glanced up at the sunlight filtering through the trees and closed her eyes to pray. "Lord Jesus, please help me to hear your beautiful voice. I need you to comfort me."

She continued praying and suddenly heard the voice of God say, "Seer, why the tears?"

His merciful voice caressed her heart, and she started sobbing heavily. "I've been accused of being clairvoyant and sexually promiscuous, my Lord."

"Why waste time meditating on dead thoughts? You belong to me. I love you, and will never leave you."

Destiny's heart was filled with joy by the power of His Word. She looked up at the rays of light and replied passionately, "I love you too, Jesus, always. Thank you for loving the pain away."

After several moments of enjoying her Lord's presence, Destiny heard Jesus say, "Seer, I want you to do something for Me."

She happily replied, "Yes, my Lord, anything."

"I want you to marry Charles."

Her eyes widened with surprise. She answered in a distressing whine, "Charles? No, I wish only to please you."

"Then marry Charles."

"But I've sworn chastity."

"That was not my will for your life."

She held her head down and started crying.

"Destiny, Charles has my Spirit just as you do. I want you to let him into your heart. He won't hurt you. I promise."

She managed a smile and said, "Yes, Lord."

22

Destiny sat in the back row of the Liberty Church staring out the window at the drops of rain splattering against the pane. She wiped what seemed to be an endless stream of tears flowing down her face. It was just before the start of the Wednesday evening service. Charles and Melissa were sitting in the pew directly across from her.

Charles stared affectionately at Destiny and queried, "I wonder what's wrong with her."

Melissa replied, "I don't know. I've never seen her so unhappy."

"Do you think I should go over and talk to her?" he inquired anxiously.

"No. I think you should leave her alone for right now."

All of a sudden, one of the warlocks from the coven walked into the main sanctuary with his wife and two children and whispered something to Elder Jackson. The Elder took a quick glance at Destiny and shook his head in confusion. Then he got out of his seat and hurried over to the Pastor who was sitting in the front row. While whispering the message into the Preacher's ear, he pointed to the family storming out of the church.

The Pastor looked very upset as he stood to his feet and faced the congregation. Holding his Bible in one hand and the microphone in the other, he said, "Church, let me have your attention for a moment."

The church instantly got quiet.

"What I have to say is not easy for me...."

Pastor Sumner eyed the young Prophetess hiding in the back row and continued talking. "But I believe you have a right to know. Recently, I received statements from several people in this church accusing Destiny of immoral and unscrupulous behavior."

Right away, the congregation began to murmur among themselves and turned around to gawk at Destiny. The Australian beauty's face turned red with embarrassment, and she lowered her head in disgrace.

Charles loudly protested under his breath, "No way! Who'd believe that?"

Melissa promptly rebuked her brother. "Charles, keep your voice down."

The Pastor raised his voice and insisted, "Please, let me finish."

The congregation quieted down, and the Pastor continued his announcement. "Tonight, another family came to Elder Jackson with the same allegation. I have already removed Destiny from her leadership position at Liberty and now publicly request that she leave this church."

Destiny began to weep copiously, her soul crying out in great pain. *Noooooo!*

Reading out of the Bible, Pastor Sumner uttered, "What is loosed on earth is loosed in heaven."

He got quiet for a moment to wipe the tears from his eyes and then continued talking, "Destiny, as head of the Liberty Church, I loose you from this congregation until you get your heart right with God.'"

Destiny was mortified when she heard the verdict and suddenly felt sick to her stomach. When she tried to stand to her feet, she almost collapsed to the floor. She cried out despondently, "Pastor, please don't expel me. Please. I promise you my heart has not turned evil."

Charles and Melissa couldn't stop the tears from coursing down their faces, listening to the cries of the belittled prophetess.

Pastor Sumner wiped his tears and turned away from Destiny.

Sobbing heavily, she continued to beg for mercy. "Please, don't turn me out. You're my family. Please."

Charles whispered angrily to Melissa, "I can't stand this anymore. I got to do something."

He started to get up but Melissa pushed him back down in his seat. She sternly commanded, "Sit down! You cannot go against the order of the church."

When Destiny saw the congregation turn away from her, she fled the main sanctuary.

Soon as Charles jumped up to go after her, Melissa grabbed him by the sleeve and whispered, "Charles, leave her alone."

"No. She needs me. I have to go to her."

23

Destiny continued bawling, standing outside under the cement awning of the church. Peering up at the dark storm-clouded sky, she watched the lightning veins flash across the heavens. When rain began to pour, she quickly made haste for her car. Little did she know, she was about to take one of the biggest moral tests of her life.

Charles ran outside and saw Destiny scurrying across the street. He shouted to the top of his lungs, "Destiny!"

She was too distraught to hear him and kept on running.

Thinking she was still rejecting him, Charles lowered his head in disillusionment and went back into the church.

Suddenly, the spirit of Baal-zebub appeared out of nowhere. He had three bee flies hovering around his head and a bee hive in his left hand. The ghostly clone grinned inhumanly at Destiny while watching her climb into her car. Then he dipped his index finger into the hive and arrogantly boasted: HONEY I'M GOING TO LOVE HOLDING YOU AGAIN.

WHEN I GET FINISHED WITH YOU, YOUR WORDS WILL TASTE SWEETER THAN HONEY IN MY MOUTH, HAHAHAHA.

Baal-zebub sucked the sugary black substance off his finger and disappeared.

The very next moment, Jeremy walked around the corner of the building with a wicked grin on his face and sauntered into the church.

Meanwhile, Destiny was still weeping heavily while driving up a hill in the pouring rain. She was having a great deal of difficulty concentrating with all of Satan's slanderous accusations buzzing around inside her head.

YOU'RE CLAIRVOYANT...CLAIRVOYANT ...CLAIRVOYANT.

"I am not clairvoyant," she screamed in utter detest.

THE CHURCH TURNED THEIR BACK ON YOU. IF I WERE YOU, I'D GET EVEN WITH THEM...GET EVEN WITH THEM...GET EVEN WITH THEM. THAT'S RIGHT, DESTINY, FEEL MY HATE...HATE...HATE.

Destiny cried out piously, "No! I will not get even with them. God is love, and in Him there is no hate, only for evil.

She closed her eyes tightly and called out to her Lord. "Jesus, help me, please. I don't want to hurt you."

Jesus reciprocated in a tender voice that echoed inside her soul, *Destiny, you must forgive...forgive...forgive.*

Satan's slanderous thoughts seemed relentless as he continued to prick her pride.

YOU'RE ALL ALONE, DESTINY. GOD HAS REJECTED YOU...REJECTED YOU...REJECTED YOU.

She squeezed her eyes tightly for a brief moment, uttering fervently, "God would never leave me nor forsake me."

HE LET THEM EXCOMMUNICATE YOU...EXCOMMUNICATE YOU...EXCOMMUNICATE YOU.

Destiny screamed with all her might, "No! That's not true!"

THINK ABOUT IT. GOD COULD HAVE STOPPED THE PASTOR FROM PUBLICLY HUMILIATING YOU IN FRONT OF THE ENTIRE CONGREGATION, BUT HE DIDN'T. AFTER ALL, NOTHING IS IMPOSSIBLE FOR GOD, RIGHT?

Destiny was so upset she almost drove off a cliff and quickly slammed her foot on the emergency break. The abrupt stop made her bang her head on the steering wheel and knocked her unconscious.

Several moments later, Destiny awoke with a big goose egg on the left side of her head. She groaned miserably, "Ooooh, my head."

She climbed out of the car feeling dizzy and staggered into the pouring rain. Peering over the edge of the cliff at the long drop below, she began to experience a touch of vertigo. Her heart was racing so fast she found it difficult to think clearly.

Once more, she cried out to her Lord, "Jesus, help me!"

Suddenly, an evil ghostly clone that looked exactly like Destiny appeared in front of her. The dark spirit grabbed her left hand and turned it over, exposing a black circular stinger embedded in the center of her palm. Pressing on the stinger, the clone buzzed its demonic thoughts into her ear.

COME BACK TO ME, DESTINY.

"Who are you?" she said fearfully.

I'M YOU IN THE PAST. SOMEONE YOU KEEP TRYING TO RUN AWAY FROM.

She glared at the image and said, "My past is dead. You no longer have any meaning to me. I live for Jesus now."

YOU CAN'T RUN FROM ME, DESTINY, I'LL ALWAYS BE THERE.

"No!"

YOU HAVE TO COME BACK TO ME. YOU HAVE NO WHERE ELSE TO GO. GOD HAS TURNED AGAINST YOU.

She wiped her tears and said fervently, "Jesus wouldn't do that. He loves me."

Thunder rumbled and lightning flashed across the sky as the clone continued humming its thoughts into her ear.

SEER, NOBODY LIKES TO BE AROUND YOU BECAUSE THEY THINK YOU'RE WEIRD. ISN'T THAT WHY YOU RUN FROM CHARLES, BECAUSE YOU'RE AFRAID HE'LL REJECT YOU TOO?

Destiny thought about Charles for a moment. Was she running from him because of fearing rejection? She didn't know if that was true or not. Then she heard Charles' pitiable cries echoing inside her soul. *Why won't you let me get close to you...close to you...close to you?*

The clone grinned fiendishly and again pressed on the stinger in her hand.

EVEN YOU'RE RICH DADDY DIED CURSING YOU, BECAUSE HE WANTED A SON.

Destiny started weeping profusely as she thought about the past. She knew her earthly father never wanted her and made that quite clear by perverting her. He constantly reminded her that his life would have been better if he'd only had a son. His emotional and physical bashings struck at the rose of her heart until he finally passed away when she was nineteen.

YOUR PAST WILL ALWAYS BE THERE TO HAUNT YOU, DESTINY. THE ONLY WAY TO GET RID OF ME IS TO JUMP. THEN ALL THE PAIN OF REJECTION WILL BE GONE FOREVER.

Destiny stared at the huge waves crashing against the rocks below, feeling like she was on an emotional roller coaster.

Once more, the clone tried to drive her over the edge by pricking her pride.

EVER SINCE THE DAY YOU WERE BORN, YOU HAD THE FEAR OF FALLING.

The ghost sneered at the prophetess and then buzzed louder into her ear.

PROVE YOU'RE NOT AFRAID, DESTINY, JUMP. IF GOD TRULY LOVES YOU, HE WILL SAVE YOU.

Destiny looked down at the long drop below and shouted, "No! God's Holy Spirit lives inside me, and I will not destroy His temple."

The very next moment, Destiny heard the sound of Jesus' thoughts speaking to her heart. *Destiny, don't let evil become a giant in your mind. Resist Satan by speaking My Word and he will vanish.*

Destiny wiped her tears and nodded. Staring into the face of darkness, she boldly proclaimed the Word of God. "No, I will not jump. For it is written, 'Do not put the Lord your God to the test.'"

Lightning flashed across the sky and thunder rumbled through the heavens as the clone screamed in a rage. "AAAAAAAAAGH!"

Suddenly, the dark ghost began to shrink smaller and smaller with every breath she uttered out of the Word of God. "God did not give me a spirit of fear. He gave me a spirit of love, power, and a sound mind."

The clone covered its ears and shouted louder.

GOD'S WORD WON'T HELP YOU FORGET THE PAST. THEY ARE JUST EMPTY WIND.

"I let go of the past and reach forward to those things in the future, my new life in Jesus Christ."

NOOOOOOO!

It wasn't long before the clone had shrunk down to the size of an insect. As Destiny continued speaking the Word of God, the clone's demonic thoughts seemed like nothing more than the insignificant buzzing of a teensy weensy fly.

"I put my trust in the Lord, and He calms the storms that come against me."

Shortly afterward, the dark ghost completely vanished.

The young Prophetess stared at the lightning striking the dark sky and smugly declared, "Death, where is your sting? Hell, where is your victory?"

Destiny suddenly awoke with her head lying on top of the steering wheel. She slowly lifted her head and groaned, "Oooooh, my head. What happened?"

Still dazed over the recent events, the Prophetess said, "I must have been having a bad dream."

Destiny looked out the window at the overhang and said, "Oh, that's right, I almost drove off the cliff."

She smiled warmly and said, "Thank you, Lord Jesus, for saving me."

24

Destiny crept quietly into the church, dripping wet, before the close of the Wednesday night service. She stopped for a moment to calm her anxiety, knowing what she had to do was not going to be easy. She slowly strode down the middle aisle, making her way towards the altar. Soon as the congregation saw her, a dead silence fell over the place. She strolled up to the Pastor and the three Elders, who were praying for people at the altar, and said affectionately with tears in her eyes, "I love you...always. You're my family."

Then she immediately turned around and walked back down the aisle. As Destiny approached the back of the church, she felt an evil presence. She stopped and glanced over at Jeremy who was hiding in the back row.

Baal-zebub's thoughts thundered through Jeremy's soul like a raving lunatic.

GET OUT OF THERE! SHE CAN SEE ME.

Although he had been warned, Jeremy was too terrified to move. His eyes were fixed with a look of dread as the Prophetess slowly came towards him.

I SAID GET OF THERE, NOW!

Melissa was shocked to see Jeremy in the church. She elbowed Charles and whispered, "Charles, I don't believe it, it's Jeremy."

Charles immediately turned around and said surprisingly, "What is he doing here?"

Destiny spoke boldly to Jeremy like a true General in the army of God. "You have allowed Beelzebub to blind your heart in order to destroy this church. But God said, 'The gates of hell will not prevail against it!'"

Suddenly, a huge hand of light overshadowed hers. Jeremy was so frightened by the hand coming towards him that his eyes started twitching. He felt like his heart was going to leap out of his chest.

DON'T LET HER TOUCH YOUR EYES.

Laying her right hand over his eyes, she sternly asserted, "And now the hand of the Lord is upon you. You shall be blind, not seeing the sun for a time."

Jeremy screamed bloody murder as she departed the sanctuary. "Help me, I'm blind! Please! I can't see! Please help me!"

The congregation just sat there in shock not moving a muscle. They were so stunned they didn't know what to do.

Charles and Melissa leaped out of their seat and hurried over to help Jeremy.

The Pastor realized he had made a huge mistake as he watched Destiny walk out the double doors. "What have I done? I was a pawn in the devil's sting. Oh Lord, please forgive me for wrongly accusing one of your seers and subjecting her to public humiliation."

Charles spoke tenderly to his friend. "Jeremy, don't be afraid, it's Charles. Let me help you."

Jeremy touched Charles' face with his fingertips and replied excitedly, "Charles is that really you?"

"Yes, little buddy, it's me. I'm here to take care of you."

Charles picked Jeremy up and quickly carried him out of the building. Pastor Sumner and Melissa followed closely behind.

Right before the Pastor exited the double doors, he turned around and said, "Ray, please let the people know that everything will be all right and close the service."

Elder Ray immediately responded, "Yes sir."

25

Jeremy looked deathly ill sitting in a rocking chair, nervously rocking back and forth in one of the spare rooms at the Pastor's house. Sleep had eluded him for days, which was evidenced by the deep dark circles that had formed around his bloodshot eyes. His skin had broken out in a cold sweat and was white as a piece of chalk. The poor thing seemed to be slipping further and further away from reality.

The door suddenly opened and Pastor Sumner walked into the room carrying a *Holy Bible*. He said with a sunny disposition, "How are you feeling, Jeremy?"

The Professor growled abhorrently at the Pastor and turned away.

"Cheer up, Jeremy. I got something that will make you feel a whole lot better."

Pastor Sumner sat down on the bed and started referring to a passage of scripture out of the *Holy Bible* from the book of Acts, Chapter 26 (NIV). "Jeremy, Jesus wants to open your eyes...."

The blind Professor immediately covered his ears and vociferously bellowed, "Shut up!"

The Pastor completely ignored Jeremy's remark and kept right on reading. "To turn them from darkness to light and from the power of Satan to God...."

Jeremy choked and coughed several times upon hearing the holy words and then immediately pulled out a handkerchief from his back pocket. Covering his nose and mouth with the cloth, he shouted in a voice of frenzy. "I said shut up! Your

God's breath is a stench in my nostrils, and I can't stand it anymore."

"So that you may receive forgiveness of sins and a place among those who are made holy by faith in Him...."

Jeremy was desperate to stifle the voice of God. He quickly felt around for an object on the table and grabbed the first thing he touched. Throwing it at the Pastor, he shouted, "Shut up, Preacher Man!"

Pastor Sumner swiftly ducked the crystal vase that came hurtling towards his head and replied, "Jeremy, don't resist the Holy Spirit. Let His words into your heart. He can help you."

"No! I hate your God. He took my eyes."

"Only to show you how blind evil has made your heart to good thoughts. Don't worry, your sight will return soon."

Jeremy cried out in desperation, "Beelzebub, save me!"

Pastor Sumner laughed and said, "You expect, Satan, the mastermind behind Baal-zebub and all the other demonic ringleaders, to save you?"

Jeremy hissed and growled vengefully at the Pastor's scoffing. He took another object off the table and threw it in his direction. The candy jar he threw caught the Pastor completely by surprise and barely missed his head as it shattered against the wall.

Once more, Jeremy shouted to the top of his lungs, "Beelzebub, save me!"

"Jeremy, don't be a fool. He's the one destroying you."

When the Professor couldn't find anything else to throw at the Pastor, his grimace quickly turned psychotic. He started ripping out hunks of his hair, screaming like a madman. "I got to stop the evil voices. They're driving me insane."

Jeremy pulled out a knife he had hidden in his pocket and tried to stab himself in the head.

"Jeremy, no!" shouted the Pastor, jumping up to grab the knife out of his hand.

The Professor growled hatefully, "Leave me alone. It's the only way to stop the pain."

"No, that's not true. Jesus can take away the pain. Renounce Satan, and receive Jesus into your heart so He can help you."

"No. You're lying. He can't help me. Nobody can."

After struggling with Jeremy to the point of exhaustion, the Pastor finally got the knife out of his hand.

Jeremy screamed frantically, "Give it back to me! I have to stop the voices."

The Pastor spoke in a tender voice, trying to calm him down. "It's okay, Jeremy, everything's going to be all right."

Jeremy threw a temper tantrum for several minutes until he finally passed out. The Pastor carried him over to the bed and gently laid his head on the pillow. After he covered him with a warm blanket, he turned out the light and closed the door.

Pastor Sumner walked into the living room shaking his head. He sighed heavily and said to Charles and Melissa who were sitting on the couch frantic with worry, "He's really sick, and I'm afraid the schizophrenia's getting worse."

"Oh no," Melissa replied sadly.

Charles put his arm around his sister to comfort her and said upsettingly, "Pastor, he's been ranting and raving ever since we brought him here two days ago. Why isn't he getting better?"

"I don't know, but we're not giving up. We're going to keep fasting and praying and speaking the Word of God until we exorcise that evil spirit out of him."

All at once, the phone rang and the Pastor answered, "Hello. Hi Destiny. Thanks for returning my call. I wanted to know if you could come over and join us in prayer on behalf of Jeremy."

"Sure, I'd love to. I'll be there soon as I can."

"All right, I'll see you when you get here. Bye."

About a half hour later, the Pastor heard a knock on the door and let Destiny in. The moment she stepped through the door his eyes welled up with tears.

Destiny said mercifully, "You don't have to say it, Pastor. I know."

Pastor Sumner smiled and gave her a hug.

Destiny glanced over at Charles and saw that he was still heartsick over their last conversation. To break the tension between them, she gave him a friendly smile and then waved to Melissa.

Melissa promptly waved back and then whispered in Charles' ear, "See, Charles, she's not mad at you. Destiny has the love of God in her heart. She would never hold a grudge."

Charles perked up and said, "That's good. I was afraid she would never speak to me again after what I did."

Destiny asked the Pastor, "Where is Jeremy?"

"He's in the spare bedroom. I'll show you where it's at."

The Pastor and Destiny tiptoed into the bedroom while Charles and Melissa followed close behind. Once inside the room, the Pastor turned on the lamp sitting on the end table.

Jeremy was still lying in bed unconscious having a great deal of difficulty breathing. Destiny put her hand on his forehead and said in a hushed tone, "His skin feels really cold."

Charles said worriedly, "Maybe we should take him to see a doctor."

Melissa promptly replied, "So they can lock him up in some institution the rest of his life? I don't know about you, Charles, but I don't know of any doctor besides Jesus that specializes in removing evil spirits."

Charles knelt down beside the bed in tears and said quietly, "Don't worry, buddy, I'm here for you."

Destiny gently patted Charles' hand to comfort him. "It will be all right, Charles. God has a perfect timetable for everything. He knows what he's doing."

The Pastor put his hand on Charles' shoulder and said, "Come on, Charles, let's go pray."

After they all sat down in the living room, they bowed their heads to pray. They had no sooner lowered their heads when they heard the sound of shattering glass. Instantly, they all jumped up and rushed to the bedroom door.

"The door's stuck. I can't get it open," the Pastor said surprisingly.

All at once, Melissa heard a loud gust of wind and the sound of flapping wings coming from behind the door. She asked fearfully, "What is that noise?"

The Pastor replied a bit shakily, "I don't know."

Charles rammed his body against the door several times and shouted, "Jeremy, can you hear me? Jeremy, open the door."

Trying to be helpful, Melissa suggested, "Why don't we get a screwdriver?"

Turning the doorknob back and forth, Charles replied, "We don't need one. See, the door isn't locked."

Destiny interjected and said, "A demonic spirit is pushing against the door, trying to keep the Word of God out of Jeremy's heart."

The Pastor prayed earnestly, "Lord, help us get the door open."

Melissa was suddenly filled with the boldness of the Holy Spirit and cried out, "Devil, we're coming in whether you like it or not. So get your hands off that door in the mighty name of Jesus!"

All at once, the door burst opened and Melissa hollered out, "Yes! Thank you, Jesus. You are my strength in time of trouble."

Pastor Sumner hurried into the room and searched for Jeremy's whereabouts. When he couldn't find him, he rushed over to the shattered picture window. The moment he leaned on the sill, a strong gust of wind shoved him backwards. After seeing a small dragonfly hovering outside the ledge, he grumbled under his breath, "You devil's darning needle. You're always trying to push against the breath of God."

Charles overheard his reproving remark and queried, "Devil's darning needle? Pastor, what is that supposed to mean?"

"It's from an old superstition where they believed the dragonfly possessed the power to sew up children's mouths while they slept. I was just thinking how Satan is like this mythical dragonfly."

"How's that?"

The Pastor picked up the *Holy Bible* off the lamp table and replied, "Satan knows all of God's children have the Word of God living inside them. Every time we speak God's Word in faith, His breath or wind comes out of us, forcing the powers of darkness to bow to the *Light*. That's why the devil tries to get the church to fall asleep spiritually. It's the only way he can sew up the mouth of God."

Charles frowned at the insect and said, "Ugh, that's sick. Melissa, get me a fly swatter will you?"

The tiny dragonfly buzzed at them several times and then darted away.

Charles looked at the Pastor and laughed, "Did you hear that? It sounded like that little bugger was laughing at us."

"So what do we do now? We don't even know where Jeremy is," inquired Melissa.

Destiny closed her eyes for a moment to pray and shortly afterward said, "Jeremy's been taken to an old abandoned shack in the marshland."

Melissa queried, "Great, where are we going to find a boat this time of night?"

"We can rent one at Outdoor Recreation," replied Charles.

Melissa checked her watch and said, "But aren't they closed already? It's eight o'clock."

"No. It's Friday night. They don't close until nine. Come on."

26

Charles and Melissa anxiously paddled the small boat down the dark eerie swamp while Destiny held the lantern to shine the way.

The ghostly shadows of the surrounding forest and the loudmouth bullfrogs intensified the spookiness of the marsh as their voices reverberated through the quagmire.

Spotting an alligator in the water, Melissa squealed, "Ugh, get away from me!"

Concerned about his sister's safety, Charles inquired, "What is it?"

Melissa tightened her lips in disgust and replied, "It's a gator."

"Don't worry. I don't think he's going to bother us," he calmly reassured her.

Meanwhile, back at the old secluded shack, Jeremy was sitting at the table looking intently through a magnifying glass at the word, "Murder," in the dictionary.

The Professor looked up for a moment at the full moon casting its shadow through the uncovered window and sighed, "Charles, I'm scared. I feel like I'm losing my mind. I can't seem to stop thinking about killing somebody. I wish you were here to help me."

Jeremy clenched his teeth tightly, looking back down at the eradicating word in the lexicon. All of a sudden, love-bugs crawled out of the dictionary and spelled the words: YOU WILL FIND A WEAPON INSIDE MY WORDS. USE IT TO KILL CHARLES.

The Professor muttered fearfully under his breath, "Kill Charles?"

Directly afterward, the tiny insects forming the letters in WORDS, unscrambled to spell the word SWORD.

Instantly, the word SWORD transformed into a dagger that looked like a small sword.

The Professor was appalled at the thought and declared boisterously, "No! I will not kill Charles. I'm going to kill you."

Jeremy angrily slammed the dictionary closed and grabbed the blade off the table. Soon as he tried to use the weapon to stab the spelling insects, his knife turned back into bugs. Infuriated by the deception, he screamed in a rage and shook the little pests out of his hand.

The moment the love-bugs fell back onto the table, they swiftly united together with the other flies and spelled out the words: *I SEE YOU ARE STILL TRYING TO UNBURY YOUR CONSCIENCE. I WARN YOU THAT COULD BE VERY PAINFUL.*

Jeremy had barely finished reading the message when he started feeling excruciating pain in his stomach. He immediately clutched his tummy and bellowed so loud his voice echoed through the swamp.

"What was that?" Melissa asked fearfully.

"It sounded like Jeremy," Charles replied anxiously.

Melissa said in a voice of panic, "Charles, he sounded like he was in a lot of pain, we got to find him."

Charles tried to set her mind at rest her while rowing the small boat down the bayou fast as he could. "Don't worry we're going to find him."

Moments later, Destiny sighted the shack up ahead and cried out, "There it is!"

Charles maneuvered the craft along side of the small dock and anchored the boat. After the three uninvited guests hurried up the stairs, Charles tried opening the door. "It's locked. I'll have to break it open."

Jeremy heard Charles' voice outside and waved his hand to open the door. "Come in, Charles, I've been expecting you."

Right away, the creaky door slowly opened, and the three guests entered the room feeling a bit apprehensive. When Melissa saw Jeremy's body covered with flies, she leaned over and whispered in Charles' ear. "Ugh, he's got ghost bugs crawling all over him, and did you see his eyes? They're glowing red like hell crawled in there with him."

Charles' mouth gaped open in astonishment. Staring intently at his friend, he whispered quietly to Destiny, "How can that be?"

"It looks like our eyes have been opened to see a metaphorical illustration of the devastating affects of choosing evil over good."

"Are we dreaming?" queried Charles.

Melissa curled up her lip in disgust at the bugs and replied, "If we are, we're all having the same nightmare."

All at once, an electric chair slid across the room and hit Charles in the back of the leg. Startled, he spun around and saw an active current in the seat.

Jeremy's prankish laughter inundated the room. "Have a seat...buddy."

Destiny glared disapprovingly at Jeremy and said, "It is written, 'You shall not kill!'"

Instantly, after she spoke the prophetic words, the seat of *"no mercy"* disappeared.

The Professor leered at the young Prophetess with a vile expression. "Get out of here. You're such a fly in the ointment."

Jeremy waved his left hand and objects in the room began to hurl at Destiny.

Fearing for her life, Charles shouted out a warning. "Destiny, look out!"

Again, Destiny's right hand was overshadowed with light, forcing each object to the ground.

Melissa leaned over to Charles and spoke just above a stifle. "If I weren't seeing this for myself, I would never believe it."

"Me either," Charles whispered back.

Jeremy was infuriated against the power she possessed. He quickly looked around for a weapon, and a knife miraculously appeared on the table. When the Professor tried to use it to stab Destiny, she waved her hand and the weapon flew out of his fingers. He screamed in an outrage watching his dagger hurl across the room.

Destiny smiled and said confidently, "God will not allow you to hurt me."

He growled with contempt in his voice, "Hurt you? Yes, I want to hurt you. After all, I am pain."

Melissa crinkled up her nose in disgust and replied with a voice of detestation, "You don't have to convince us you're a pain."

Jeremy immediately retaliated by using his demonic powers to summon the knife back into his hand. Growling like a ravenous wolf, he boasted, "I'm going to kill you Charles!"

Charles raised his voice out of annoyance and said, "Jeremy, stop acting like a turd! We came here to help you."

"Remember, Charles, I'm beyond help."

Charles whispered into Destiny's ear, "How did he know I said that?"

"The evil spirit's telling him," she whispered back.

"Oh, that's right."

Jeremy stared at his unwanted guests like they were nothing more than insects he was studying. "You humans should thank me."

"For what?" Charles snapped sarcastically.

Jeremy smirked and said, "If we hadn't got you to sin, you could never feel us."

The Professor lifted his knife into the air and stabbed himself in the left hand.

Melissa squealed with fright as she watched the blood pouring out of Jeremy's hand.

Jeremy laughed like a fiend and said, "What's the matter Melissa? Don't you like the way we make you feel?"

The Professor waved his hand and the wound quickly disappeared. Then he sat back down at the table.

Charles sneered at Jeremy and queried, "What's with this we? And what's with all the love-bugs?"

Melissa leaned over to her brother and spoke quietly. "Those black flies crawling all over him are called love-bugs?"

Charles nodded.

"Ugh! What could an evil spirit possibly love?" she said annoyingly.

Jeremy grinned wickedly at Melissa and said, "To express myself."

Destiny was sick of the devil's voice polluting the room and boldly commanded, "Nobody cares what an evil spirit has to say."

"If that were true, the voice of evil would have been silenced a long time ago."

The young prophetess glared in the demon's direction and strongly demanded, "In the holy name of Jesus, I command you evil spirit to shut up!"

Instantly, Jeremy's head fell forward and thumped on top of the table.

Charles snickered, "I bet Jeremy's going to have a seriously bad headache when he wakes up out of this nightmare."

He grabbed the knife out of Jeremy's hand and tossed it out the window.

Melissa raised her voice and said, "Hey, Charles, come here for a minute and look at this."

Soon as her brother walked over, Melissa pointed to three ghostly bee flies disappearing into Jeremy's forehead. "Isn't that disgusting?"

He replied with a look of distaste. "It sure is. The way these phantom flies are attracted to his mind you'd think he had you know what for brains."

Charles fanned his right hand rapidly to scare away the ghostly love-bugs crawling all over Jeremy. "Go on, shoo, get off him!"

While lifting Jeremy's head to examine him, Charles accidentally dropped it back on the table. He said with a goofy expression, "Whoops, sorry buddy. I think I just turned your headache into a migraine, heeheehee."

Melissa stared nauseatingly at the three love-bugs crawling out of Jeremy's head. "Hey, Destiny, what do you think the three flies symbolize?"

"I think the ring of flies is supposed to represent the insignificant voice of Satan that continually murmurs against the united voice of God the Father, God the Son, and God the Holy Spirit."

"Really?"

She nodded. "Satan's counterfeit ring continually opposes the guarantee of our true inheritance which is the Holy Spirit Himself. You might find it interesting that the Greek word for *"guarantee"* can also be used to indicate an engagement or promise ring, especially since Jesus represents the Bridegroom, and the church represents the bride.

"I don't quite understand," replied Melissa.

Destiny set the lantern down on the table and continued to elaborate. "After the bride gave her heart to the Bridegroom by putting her faith in Him, she said, "I will."

Then the Bridegroom sealed the marriage agreement by giving His betrothed the ring of His Holy Spirit as a guarantee that one day her soul would be completely joined to His Holiness."

Melissa acted like she was on cloud nine after hearing the metaphorical illustration and said, "That is so beautiful. Just imagine…never being able to think another evil thought again."

27

Without warning, a strong gust of wind blew through the window and put out the light in the lamp.

"Hey, Melissa, turn on that light overhead," said Charles.

"Okay," she replied and then turned on the black light above the table.

Soon as the room flooded with black light, Melissa shrunk back and shrieked, "Oh my goodness. Charles, look at Jeremy's skin, it's covered in black rings."

"You got to be kidding me," he uttered dismayingly and then started examining Jeremy under the black light.

"What is that?" Destiny inquired in a repulsive tone.

Charles replied, "I don't know. I've never seen ringworm like that before."

Destiny picked up the magnifying glass off the table and peeped through the glass at one of the dark circles on Jeremy's body. Horrified by what she saw, she gasped and quickly covered her mouth.

"Destiny, what's wrong?" Charles asked restlessly.

Still stunned, Destiny slowly handed Charles the magnifying glass without uttering a word.

Charles' facial expression changed to a look of astonishment when he peeked through the glass. "It can't be."

"Charles, what is it?" Melissa queried fearfully.

He scratched the side of his head, feeling a bit perturbed. "It has to be trick glass."

Charles decided to take a closer look.

Melissa shouted impatiently, "Charles!"

When he still didn't acknowledge her, she snatched the magnifying glass out of his hand to see what was going on. Peering through the glass, Melissa saw a black ring on Jeremy's skin formed out of the words, HATE, REVENGE, and CURSE. She said loudly, "No way!"

She held the magnifying glass over another black ring and saw the words, LIE, CHEAT, and DECEIVE. After seeing a similar pattern, Melissa excitedly uttered, "Charles, look at this."

Peeking through the glass, he queried, "What is it?"

"Don't you see it? All the words are traveling in the same circle."

Charles stared hard through the glass at one of the black rings and saw the words, EVIL, CORRUPT, and SIN. He wiped his dry mouth with his hand and said, "Oh man that is so weird. Talk about wearing your heart on your sleeve. Saint Paul sure knew what he was talking about when he said that in our flesh dwells no good thing, and if we give ourselves over to our sinful nature we will be controlled by it."

Destiny said joyfully, "Aren't you glad God gave us his Holy Spirit so we can use his words (*sword*) to put these sinful thoughts to death?"

"Yeah, with God's thoughts living inside of us, we can now travel in a different circle."

While Charles continued talking to Destiny, Melissa instinctively turned the magnifying glass over and peeked through the other side.

When Charles noticed his sister was acting peculiar, he inquired, "Melissa, you look bug-eyed. What's the matter with you?"

Melissa cupped her hand over her mouth and handed the magnifying glass back to Charles. "I think I'm going to throw up."

Destiny leaned over Charles' shoulder to peep through the glass and groaned, "Ugh, maggots."

Staring intently at one of the ghostly ring of worms, he said, "If I didn't know better, I'd swear these words are using him as some sort of medium."

Melissa blurted out, "You got to be kidding me. That's disgusting!"

"I know it is, but apparently, in order for these words to finish their morphogenesis, they have to worm their way into his belly, which is merely symbolic for a place of spiritual digestion."

Charles looked up at Melissa and added, "It looks like they plan on using him as a dummy to express themselves in the earth."

"Let me get this straight. Are you trying to tell me that Jeremy and these words are becoming one?"

Charles nodded and replied, "I think so."

"How is that possible?"

Destiny cut in and said, "Jeremy has a stomach for evil, and anything you digest…."

Melissa promptly interrupted. "You become one with."

Charles lifted Jeremy's shirt and pointed at his belly. "Look at the words burned into his stomach."

Melissa turned up her nose and said, "Sick!"

"See what I mean. Evil desires to speak."

Charles pulled down Jeremy's shirt and said sorrowfully, "Jeremy's now what you'd call a "fly-by-night.""

"A fly-by-night? What's that?"

"A shady person…you know…someone you can't trust."

"Oh."

Charles peered back into the glass and commented, "Whatever's going on inside his mind, has definitely gone beyond the early developmental stage."

Destiny looked at Charles and said, "When you think about it, it makes perfect sense. If the human race stopped believing in lies, they would quit telling them."

Charles felt elated by her words and said, "Yeah then the word liar and its sect would die."

Melissa grinned from ear to ear and added, "And its spirit would be gone forever."

Destiny peeped through the glass and said, "Seeing the spirit behind these words as nothing but a low-life maggot makes you realize just how morally blind Satan can make us if we start craving his thoughts."

"Yeah since a maggot has no eyes, and we all know what it feeds on," Charles chuckled.

Melissa stared at the worms and said, "If the maggot is a metaphorical representation of a person that's morally blind, and light represents the truth, how come these words appear iridescent under the black light?"

Destiny replied, "The shine isn't genuine. It doesn't come from within. Satan appears that way outwardly to deceive people into thinking he reflects light. But on the inside, he's a carrier of darkness; or to put it more plainly, a carrier of moral disease. I guess you could call it a *black light*. Now you see why we need the Holy Spirit to encircle our heart."

Melissa promptly responded with a smile. "Yeah, He's like a giant bug zapper. He guards it from being eaten alive every time evil comes to bug us."

Charles chuckled at his sister's metaphorical illustration. Then he turned the magnifying glass over and peered through the glass. When he saw the words, MURDER and KILL, he said to Destiny, "Look at this."

Destiny looked intently at the decimating words and said, "The ring's not connected all the way."

Charles sighed in relief and said, "At least we know he hasn't killed anybody…yet. Unfortunately, it looks like the morphogenetic process has developed into phase three."

"What do you mean?" asked Melissa.

"I guess you could compare the metamorphosis of the fly to how sin can change the way a human thinks."

"How's that?"

"Well, imagine the fly's egg represents the evil thought implanted into Jeremy's mind, such as in this case, murder. Obviously, he's thought about it long enough so it had a chance to grow and wormed its way into his heart. The third stage, which he's currently in, is called the "Pupa," where his thoughts are now encased and literally being transformed into a murderer. Then after the breaking down process is completed, the fourth and final stage of development is carried out by the act of murder."

Charles peered through the glass again and said, "Hey you guys look at this."

Destiny and Melissa immediately looked through the glass and saw a circle of maggots transforming into a ghostly bee fly.

Melissa groaned loudly, "That is so disgusting."

Charles stared at the bee fly and said, "Look at all the infestation inside its body."

Melissa replied sadly, "Poor Jeremy, he's really becoming an abomination. Does that mean his mind is now completely taken over by the spirit of hate?"

Charles looked sorrowfully at Melissa and nodded. "I'm afraid so. It looks like the metamorphical process has reached maturity and now haunts his soul."

28

Melissa picked up the gray-covered unholy bible off the table. Looking curiously at the title and the three interconnected black rings on the cover, she sighed disappointingly, "Jeremy, I don't understand how you could give your heart to this...this...evil ringleader."

Thumbing through the blank pages of the book, she added, "Who definitely can't keep his word."

Without warning, Jeremy woke up and snatched the magnifying glass out of Charles' hand. Startled by his sudden movement, Melissa screamed and dropped the book.

Jeremy sneered at Charles while holding the magnifying glass over his left eye. "So you think you've got it all figured out, huh, Sherlock?"

"Jeremy, how could you allow this to happen?"

Jeremy set the magnifying glass down on the table and smiled impishly, "Let's just say I was swept off my feet."

Still teed off, Charles snarled, "I can't believe you sold your soul to the devil. What did the lord of the flies promise you Jeremy? Riches beyond your wildest dreams, power, or was it sex?"

Jeremy's lustful eyes sparked with greed. "I got them all, buddy. See, dreams do come true."

Charles peered around the room at all the phantom bugs and chuckled in a sarcastic voice. "This is your dreams...buddy. Looks more like a nightmare to me."

Jeremy picked up a book of matches off the shelf and lit the lantern. After turning off the black light, he blew out the match. "Come on, Charles, join us, and I'll share it all with you. Don't you want the power to be a lord of the flies?"

"You blind fool! You gave up the true treasure for a pile of dust. Don't you get it, Jeremy? All your worldly treasures will one day turn back into dust. But the gift of eternal life, which is Jesus Christ, will never die."

Jeremy flicked a ghost bee fly that flew out of his forehead and said haughtily, "You humans are so pathetic. Where would you be without us? We make the man."

"Us? We? Jeremy, what the…h…are you talking about?" Charles queried grouchily.

Jeremy grinned sinisterly from ear to ear and replied, "Hell is exactly what I'm talking about, buddy. And I noticed you deliberately refrained from using that colorful metaphor. What's up?"

Charles looked over at Melissa and said, "I'm trying to cut down."

"You're trying to cut down, hahahaha. You always could make me laugh, Charles. I don't know who you're kidding. You might as well have said the "h" word, because the rest of us knew exactly what you meant."

Charles glared at Jeremy and said, "You didn't answer my question. What's with this "we" stuff?"

Jeremy's eyes glowed fiery red with hate. "Let…us… make man in our image."

All of a sudden, ghostly maggots appeared in Jeremy's hands.

Melissa made a sour face at the worms and said with distaste, "Ugh, Jeremy, you need help. You're sick."

"If I were you, Melissa, I'd close my mouth unless you plan on catching some flies."

The Professor laughed cruelly at her while the larva in his hands swiftly transformed into evil words: MURDERERS,

LIARS, THIEVES, BLASPHEMERS, FORNICATORS, MOLESTERS, SLANDERERS, PORNOGRAPHERS, DRUNKS, ADULTERERS, ADDICTS, CONCEIT, CHEATERS, VIOLENCE, SELFISHNESS, GREED, HATE AND DEATH.

"Let there be idolaters everywhere...murderers, liars, thieves, blasphemers, fornicators, molesters, slanderers, pornographers, drunks, adulterers, addicts, conceit, cheaters, violence, selfishness, greed, hate, death, and all of their kind."

The instant Jeremy finished speaking the immoral words they changed into dark ghostly images that looked exactly like him.

Charles spoke to Destiny in a hushed tone. "I think the poor soul needs to get a new image."

Destiny nodded and said with affirmation, "Definitely."

Continuing his worthless boasting, Jeremy said, "And let them multiply and fill the earth. I am their father, and they are my sons. The spirit of these words must live. In order to do that, they need a voice, someone to perform their unrighteous thoughts."

Charles picked up the demonic book off the floor and stared at the three rings on the cover. He laughed profusely and then threw the book at Jeremy, speaking with a superior attitude. "Sounds like a three-ring circus to me...buddy."

Jeremy scowled at Charles while the images in his hands miraculously turned into ghostly black seeds. Then the Professor turned his head to lustfully eyeball the young Prophetess. "Desire me, Destiny, and I will discharge my seed into your heart."

Destiny laughed chidingly. "Desire you? I'm not going to crawl on my belly and eat dust. Get behind me, Satan."

Charles jumped in and said sarcastically, "Yeah. You're thoughts are beneath our feet."

Destiny pointed at Jeremy and continued uttering, "Through the power of suggestion, you mislead the human mind into thinking you are the voice of God so man will turn away from what is real and worship you. But those of us who have Jesus living in our hearts know the truth, and His voice alone we follow."

Infuriated by her loyalty to God, Jeremy bit his lower lip until the blood oozed down his chin. Then he picked up the magnifying glass off the table and held it over his left eye. Sneering at Destiny, he inquired maliciously, "Tell me something, Seer. When your God looks at you through his magnified eye, what do you suppose he sees…a little love-bug?"

Destiny smiled and said, "I imagine when God looks at His church, He sees His offspring, children of light. We put our faith in His words. Not empty promises."

The young Prophetess reached out and took one of the seeds out of his hand. She opened the casing to show him there was nothing inside but black dirt. "Time to wake up, Jeremy. Satan's dirty kingdom is nothing but dust, it's fools gold."

The Australian beauty slapped the rest of the phantom seeds out of Jeremy's hands, and the seeds slowly vanished.

Jeremy glared his evil spirited eyes at Destiny and snarled, "I hate you, Seer!"

"Leave her alone, Jeremy," Charles snapped insistently.

While still keeping her eye on Jeremy, Destiny boldly commanded, "Charles, God said it's time to cast that evil spirit out of your friend."

Charles replied fearfully in a mousy voice, "Me?"

Melissa pushed her scared stiff brother towards Jeremy and said excitedly, "All right, Charles, go shake the dust off your feet."

Trembling from head to toe, Charles slowly inched his way over to his friend until the evil spirit inside Jeremy nastily whispered, "If you cast me out of him, I'll come into you."

Charles was panic-stricken after hearing the evil spirit's threats and quickly shrunk back. He was so scared he thought he was going to faint dead on the floor. Then he heard Jesus' reassuring voice speaking tenderly to his heart, "Charles, don't let that devil deceive your mind. He cannot inhabit your body for it is a place where I dwell."

Charles smiled knowing the truth and stood his ground.

Jeremy laughed at his friend and said, "Charles, you are such a wimp. Why you couldn't cast out a teensy fly, hahahaha."

Turning his evil aggression towards Destiny, Jeremy snarled, "Seer, I'm going to enjoy squishing you like a bug."

The Professor snatched one of the love-bugs out of the air and squashed it in his left hand. "For I know the thoughts that I think towards you...thoughts of evil and not good to take away your hope and your future."

Suddenly, Charles was filled with boldness by the power of the Holy Spirit. He pointed his right index finger toward Jeremy and bellowed, "In the mighty name of Jesus, I command you evil spirit to come out of him!"

"No!" the Professor shrieked.

Before Jeremy had time to utter another sound, a powerful stream of electricity bolted out of Charles' finger and struck the Professor in the chest, knocking him across the floor.

Jeremy immediately went into convulsions when the evil spirit resisted being expelled. His body twitched and jerked uncontrollably on the floor. When he saw Charles pointing towards the dictionary, he squealed half crazed out of his mind. "Noooo, stop!"

Charles paid no attention to his ranting as another bolt of lightning shot out of his finger and struck the lexicon.

Jeremy screamed bloody murder and then passed out after the Holy Spirit drove the demonic force out of his body.

Melissa couldn't believe her eyes. She just stood there dumbfounded, watching all the evil vocabulary flying out of the dictionary and affixing themselves to the walls like wallpaper. After the words stopped coming out the lexicon, she walked over to the table and picked it up. Flipping through the pages of the book she said, "Destiny, Charles, look at this. All the evil words are gone."

Charles glanced at several blank sections in the book where evil words and their meaning had been removed. "That's amazing. I love the way God expels evil out of the vocabulary of the heart. Once removed, it no longer has any meaning."

Melissa smiled and said happily, "Yeah."

Destiny glared at all the corrupted words trembling on the walls and said, "Dust you are and to dust you shall return."

A few seconds later, a multitude of agonizing screams could be heard in the room as the hellish words began to burn. In a desperate attempt to escape obliteration, some of the words leaped off the wall and landed on Jeremy's body. The moment the Professor felt the weight of the words stomping up and down on his chest, he awoke. Seeing evil crawling all over him, he brushed his body vigorously, screaming in a voice of delirium. "Aaaaaagh! Get off me! Get off! Somebody, get them off me!"

All at once, the cabin began to quake, and one of the rafters fell to the floor. Charles jumped out of the way of the falling debris and bellowed in a voice of fright, "We better get out of here!"

Destiny grabbed the lantern off the shaky table right before it hit the floor and shouted back, "Okay!"

Melissa hurried over to Jeremy and hollered, "Charles, help me get Jeremy into the boat!"

The very next moment, a two-by-four hit the floor directly in front of Charles. He shouted above all the commotion, "I'll get him! You girls get out of here!"

Melissa was terrified her brother might be killed trying to save Jeremy. She started sobbing loudly, "No, I'm not leaving you."

When a huge hunk of the burning wall collapsed on to the floor and barely missed taking out his sister, Charles shouted in a voice of desperation, "Destiny, please, get her out of here!"

Charles was getting ticked off with his friend who had just kicked him the face when he tried to grab him. "Oooooh, that hurt. Jeremy, stop it, quit kicking me!"

Melissa pulled hard on her brother's arm, still weeping. "I'm not going without you."

Charles pushed his sniveling sister away and shouted, "Go on, get out of here!"

He was getting a bit frustrated trying to deal with both his sister and his friend who was still ranting and raving like a lunatic.

Melissa blubbered, "No. I want to stay and help you."

"If you want to help me, Melissa, go out and pray."

Destiny said compassionately, "Charles is right. Come on, Melissa, let's go out in the boat and pray."

The young Prophetess put her arm around Charles' distraught sister and escorted her out of the shack.

Charles was relieved the girls were out of danger. Now he could focus his full attention on rescuing his hysterical friend. "Jeremy, stop kicking me. Let me help you. We got to get out of here."

He reached down to grab Jeremy and started coughing and choking on the smoke filling the room.

Jeremy just kept shouting over and over with a look of hysteria, "Get them off me! Get them off!"

Charles hacked again several times and said in a hoarse voice, "Jeremy, stop it. The words aren't real. They're only phantoms in your mind, appearing to be real."

Finally, after several attempts, Charles got a good grip on his friend and dragged him out of the shack by the seat of his pants, still kicking and screaming like a lunatic. "Jeremy, quit fighting me before you get us both killed!"

Once outside, Jeremy looked up catatonically at the stars and suddenly passed out. Charles heaved a huge sigh of relief and picked him up.

29

When Melissa heard her brother coming down the steps, she opened her eyes that she had closed during prayer and quickly spun around in the boat. Relieved to see Charles still alive, she wiped the tears from her face and said gratefully, "Thank you, God."

As Charles carried his friend over to the boat, his sister inquired, "Charles is Jeremy alright?"

Looking back at the burning shack filled with smoke, he coughed heavily and said, "He'll be fine, but we got to get out of here, fast."

Destiny held the lantern while Charles put Jeremy into the boat. After all the passengers were safely inside, Charles launched the small craft away from the dock.

The young Prophetess rested Jeremy's head on her lap and said a quick prayer over him. Then she glanced up to admire the full moon that was casting its reflection on top of the water.

After the boat was only a few yards away, Charles and Melissa noticed the shack was rapidly expanding. Right away, they both started rowing the boat fast as they could.

Melissa shouted, "Faster, Charles, faster! The shack's going to explode any second."

Melissa looked back over her shoulder at the cabin and started crying, "Charles, we're not going to make it."

Destiny closed her eyes, praying fervently. "Jesus, please save us."

All at once, she felt a gentle breeze blowing on her face, and the sound of Jesus' familiar voice speaking to her soul. "Destiny, don't let fear overcome you. Use the authority I have given you in my name, for everything I have is yours."

Destiny nodded and the words she had previously digested out of the Word of God began to flow out of her belly. "God did not give me a spirit of fear. He gave me a spirit of power, love, and a sound mind. He holds me safe in His right hand. He is my refuge and strength, a very pleasant help in time of trouble."

Before she could utter another prophetic word, the cabin exploded and disbursed thousands of sparks into the air that looked like dancing jewels, sparkling under the twilight. But before the flying debris could hit any of the passengers, God's hand of protection was there to overshadow the boat.

Charles heaved a huge sigh of relief as he watched chunks of burning wood stop just short of pelting him in the face. Then he watched what was left of the shack slowly sink into the swamp.

Happy to be alive, they all lifted their voices in one accord, singing and praising God for protecting them from evil. When they had finished singing, Destiny ripped a piece of material from the bottom of her mid-length dress and dipped it into the swamp. The moment she wiped Jeremy's brow with the wet cloth, he woke up and started screaming.

"Jeremy, calm down, everything's going to be all right," Charles reassured him.

The Professor's eyes looked like they were going to pop out of their sockets, staring catatonically at the stars. He shouted frightfully, "Oh my goodness! There must be billions of them!"

Charles looked up towards heaven and said curiously, "Billions of what?"

"Can't you see them?"

"See what? I don't know what you're babbling about."

Jeremy replied with a look of gloom, "Fireflies, don't you see them?"

Charles took another quick peek at the stars and said, "No."

The Professor started rambling with paranoia in his voice. "He sent all the fireflies in the universe after us. There's no way out. We're trapped, like flies on flypaper."

Melissa giggled and whispered in Charles' ear. "Jeremy must have gotten some stardust in his eyes. He thinks the stars are fireflies."

Charles chuckled under his breath and said, "Oh."

Jeremy squealed in a voice of terror, "They're going to attack us any minute! We got to get out of here, fast!"

Melissa snickered, "I think he hit his head harder than we thought."

Destiny wiped the perspiration from Jeremy's brow and said softly, "Don't be afraid, Jeremy, we're here to help you."

Jeremy sat up in the boat as if waking up from a nightmare. After peering fearfully in Destiny's face, he quickly moved to the other side of the boat. "Don't touch me. You stay away from me."

"She's not going to hurt you, Jeremy," said Charles.

Jeremy made a nervous gesture by rubbing the back of his neck and then slowly looked around at his immediate surroundings. "How did I get out here?"

Melissa replied, "God sent us to rescue you."

Jeremy stared puzzlingly at Destiny. "I don't understand. Why would your God help me after what I tried to do to Him?"

Destiny smiled with a twinkle in her eyes and replied, "Because He loves you."

"He loves me?" he replied sarcastically.

She nodded, still smiling.

The Professor held the sides of his head, groaning loudly, "Oooooh, I have a terrible migraine."

He gently touched the tender spot on his forehead and flinched from the pain. "Ow! Where did I get that lump on my forehead?"

Melissa snickered quietly under her breath and then replied sympathetically, "Oh, you poor thing. I wonder how that happened."

She stared smugly at Charles, and he guiltily cleared his throat.

When Charles saw his friend fidgeting uncomfortably in his seat, he queried, "What's wrong, Jeremy?"

Jeremy looked around at the ghost-like shadows in the forest and started nervously biting his fingernails. "He's not going to let me go you know."

"Who?"

The Professor stared back at the starlit sky and snapped fearfully, "Baal-zebub, that's who. He'll come after me."

Charles leaned over to Destiny and whispered confoundedly, "Why does he believe Baal-zebub will come after him. Wasn't he driven back into the desert?"

Destiny whispered back, "Demonic spirits have been known to try and regain possession of the person they've been cast out of if that person is willing to allow them back in."

Charles kept his tone quiet, making a sarcastic remark. "Great! That means Jeremy sees himself as a worm, even lower than a fly."

Melissa quickly interrupted their conversation with a voice of distress. "Oh, Charles, I sure hope you brought a big fly swatter."

"Why?"

His sister pointed uneasily in the direction of a huge swarm of bee flies and fireflies heading toward the boat. "Because we're going to need one, that's why."

Charles was horror-struck when he saw the view of the full moon darkened by a plague of insects. He replied with a taste of fear on his tongue, "Sis, I don't think they make them that big. My goodness, there must be millions of them."

When the angry insects got dangerously close to the boat, Melissa shrieked, "Aaaaaaagh! Get away from me!"

The fireflies quickly spelled out the words: THE SEER IS MINE. GIVE HIM BACK, OR I'LL KILL YOU.

Charles jeered at the intimidating words and shouted boldly, "No!"

Jeremy spouted worriedly, "He means it, buddy."

"I'm not afraid of him!" Charles replied indignantly.

"Charles, don't be stupid. Let me go, or he'll kill you."

"No! You belong with us."

Melissa pointed at the fireflies and giggled, "Charles, look at that. Every time Jeremy speaks, their little butts light up. You'd think they were in love."

Full of pride, the Professor shouted angrily in her face. "That's a lie!"

But the fireflies proved him wrong by emitting light as he spoke. Jeremy was so humiliated he slapped his hand over his mouth to stop himself from speaking.

Melissa remarked arrogantly, "See."

The fireflies quickly spelled the words: I SAID GIVE HIM BACK. HE'S MINE.

Charles raised his voice in anger, "What do I got to do, spell it out for you? The answer is N...O, now buzz off!"

Melissa felt on edge listening to the angry drones made by the bee flies, which was getting so loud it was almost deafening to the ears. "Oh guys, we better get out of here. I think lover boy's about to fly into a rage."

Jeremy made a nasty face at Melissa, showing his disapproval of her remark about him being Baal-zebub's immoral lover.

Charles said to his sister, "I think you're right."

But the moment Charles and Melissa tried to row the boat the pesky little insects circled the craft.

Melissa stared at the angry buzzing bee flies and whined, "Lord, we need some help here... Lord."

Destiny began to prophesy the Word of God with great passion. "Though we go through the fire, we will not get burned. My God will be a shield of protection all around us. He causes our enemies to flee before us. The gates of hell will not prevail against us."

Melissa stared wide-eyed at the circle of flies buzzing around the boat. "Lord Jesus, I agree with everything she just said. I know you're never late, but just this once could you get here a little earlier? You see, we got these bug things after us. Remember, you said that if we called upon your name, you'd save us. So I'm calling...collect."

The annoying pests quickly spelled out the word, "*DEATH.*"

Melissa laughed in jest, "You idiot! You spelled the word wrong again. Life is spelled...:..L...I...F...E. Of course a real spelling bee would know that."

Suddenly, Melissa heard the whistling wind and then a bright shimmering light appeared. Out of the light came thousands of glowing honey bees. When the rival insects heard the angry protective buzzing of the bees, they immediately pulled back.

In the meantime, the honey bees swiftly formed three giant circles around the boat, one directly above the other with the bottom ring resting on top of the water.

Then the passengers heard a whistle that thundered through the heavens, summoning more honey bees that came in droves. The luminous honey bees quickly filled in the gaps between each ring so that nothing could get passed them. The glowing bees looked like a huge wall of fire all around the boat.

Melissa gleefully shouted, "Yes. I knew you'd come. Our God is a wall of fire all around us. He is our shield of protection. Thank you, Jesus."

Charles whispered to Destiny, "I don't understand, why the bee?"

"Lexigraphers believe the Hebrew name for bee is derived from a root word meaning, '*to speak.*'"

"Because of the humming noise made by the bees?" queried Charles.

"Possibly," replied Destiny.

Unexpectedly, the opposing army of insects circled around the huge wall of honey bees, about twenty feet away. Their drumming got so loud that the passengers had to cover their ears.

Charles shouted to Jeremy, "What are they doing?"

"They're getting ready to attack. You should have turned me over, buddy. Why risk your own life for me."

"Give me a break, Jeremy. How could I call myself your friend if I turn my back on you?"

"That's right, and our friend, Jesus Christ, won't turn His back on us either," Melissa said full of faith.

Just then, the passengers heard a loud whistle, and the angry swarm of insects charged the wall. But the honey bees acted like a giant bug zapper and stung all the hostile insects to death.

Charles asked Destiny in a puzzled voice, "They knew it was suicide to attack the protective barrier after thousands of them were killed. So why did they keep coming towards the light knowing it would destroy them?"

She replied, "Because darkness, even in its darkest hour, never quits trying to put the light under its feet."

While watching the honey bees scrambling to spell words, Charles remarked, "But we know that's impossible."

LIFE ...I LOVE YOU...CHOOSE YOUR WORDS WISELY.

Soon as the honey bees finished spelling the words, they reassembled themselves into a huge clock.

Jeremy scratched his head and queried, "I don't get it. Why is your God spelling time?"

Destiny smiled and said, "Because Jesus wants you to spend time with him."

Jeremy stared hard at the clock. "But the time is not set. How am I supposed to know what time to spend with Him when there are no hands on the clock?"

Melissa chuckled and said, "God is not chained to time."

She gazed up at the universe for a moment and continued uttering, "He's timeless and will spend all the time you want with him."

Melissa elbowed Charles and discreetly tilted her head towards Jeremy who was busy staring at the stars.

Charles asked in a barely audible voice, "What?"

"Go on, ask him," whispered Melissa.

"He's just going to laugh at me again."

Melissa pleaded earnestly under her breath. "Charles, Jesus can't help him if you keep His voice buried in your heart. Don't let this opportunity slip through your fingers."

Charles glanced inconspicuously over at Jeremy, picking nervously at his bottom lip. Swallowing his pride, he cleared his throat and said, "Jeremy, you thought about asking Jesus into your heart once when I shared his Holy Spirit with you. What made you change your mind?"

Shrugging his shoulders uncaringly, he said, "I don't know."

Melissa butted in on their conversation and said, "It's not too late, you know. You can still ask him."

She peered up at the huge clock in the sky and added, "God is the only one who can reset the heart for eternity."

Jeremy laughed and said sarcastically, "Join my heart to a holy God. Are you kidding me? Baal-zebub would rather see me dead first. Besides, I'm nothing but a worthless speck of dust."

"That's true. Man is nothing but a speck of dust without the voice of God. But if you give Him your grain of sand, He'll breathe life into it, turning it into a beautiful pearl."

Charles leaned his elbow on Jeremy's shoulder and said, "Hey, buddy, have you ever noticed how evil always leaves a bad taste in your mouth?"

He sighed heavily and said, "Okay...buddy...I'll think about it."

Jeremy smiled in awe watching the bee-formed clock heading in the right direction. "Time really does fly by, doesn't it?"

Charles grinned and nodded.

30

When they arrived at the other side of the swamp, the passengers climbed out of the boat and pulled the vessel to shore.

Jeremy hurried towards the dark woodlands, shouting over his shoulder, "I'll be back in a minute!"

Melissa picked up the lantern out of the boat and held it up in the air, yelling, "Hey Jeremy, where you going?"

"I got to go."

"Where?"

Jeremy gave her a funny look.

Melissa felt embarrassed when she realized he was talking about going to the bathroom and said, "Oh. Do you want the lantern?"

"No. I'm used to doing it in the dark," Jeremy laughed and disappeared into the woods.

Melissa snickered while watching Charles stare at Destiny like a love-sick puppy. She elbowed her brother and spoke in a muffled voice, "Go on, you still got one strike left."

"You'd love to see me strike out wouldn't you? Just so you could say, I told you so."

Melissa giggled under her breath.

Charles continued jabbering, "Well, it just so happens that I've decided to use my last strike to ask her to marry me."

"Marry you? Are you nuts?"

"If I am, you're to blame. You're the one who makes me eat two peanut butter sandwiches with out any jelly for breakfast everyday."

"It's not my fault I don't know how to cook. You should be thanking me instead of complaining."

"For what?"

"For fixing you a breakfast that *"sticks"* with you all day, heeheehee."

Charles stuck his tongue out at his sister and headed towards Destiny.

Melissa tried to stop her brother by pulling on his arm. "Charles, don't do it. I love you too much to see you make a fool out of yourself."

He pulled away from her, grabbing the lantern out of her hand, and kept on walking.

Chasing after him, Melissa said, "But she hardly even knows you."

"So what, God gave me a Word, and that's good enough for me."

"She hasn't shown any interest in you at all. Are you sure God said you would marry Destiny? Or was it your own desires you heard?"

Charles stopped walking and got close to her face. "Melissa, wake up and have a clue. The devil is using your tongue right now to try and fill my head with doubt, and you don't even know he's doing it."

"I resent that remark!"

"It's true."

"Charles, give me a break. Destiny's been rejecting you ever since she found out you liked her. And now you think just because you ask her to marry you, she's going to say yes, hahahaha. Oh please, that is so ridiculous."

"Forget it, Melissa. I'm not letting that crafty devil steal God's Word out of my heart and leave me to eat dust!"

Charles stormed off in the direction of Destiny.

"All right, fine, go ahead, make a fool of yourself. Strike out, see if I care. When Destiny benches you, don't come crying to me!"

Melissa shook her head in frustration and sighed, "Men."

Charles walked up to Destiny and nervously looked into her eyes. His palms began to sweat profusely as his heart beat faster and faster. After swallowing his pride, he said, "Destiny, will you…uh…um…will you…um."

The more he tried to spit out what he wanted to say, the sicker he felt.

Melissa snuck up behind a tree to eavesdrop on her brother's conversation. Upon hearing her brother stumbling over his words, she snickered under her breath, "Charles, have you no pride?"

When Charles couldn't find the words he wanted to say, he lowered his head in despair, mumbling softly, "I can't do this."

Destiny was moved with compassion and gently lifted his head. After staring warmly into his tearful eyes, she smiled and said, "Charles…I will."

Charles' mouth instantly dropped open. He couldn't believe his ears and excitedly uttered, "If I'm dreaming, don't wake me up."

Melissa was totally flabbergasted by Destiny's answer and whispered loudly, "What?"

Just when Charles thought everything was going great, Destiny suddenly started groaning as if she was in a great deal of pain.

"Destiny, what's the matter?" Charles asked worriedly.

Destiny did not answer him. She was busy peering into a dark place to see a vision of six warlocks dressed in black, hiding behind trees with pistols in their hands. The instant Jeremy passed by, the warlocks circled him. After seeing the weapons in their hands, he became deafly afraid, and his heart started beating like a scared rabbit. Not knowing what to do, he started pleading for his life. "Please, don't kill me. Please, I don't want to die."

The warlocks completely ignored his cries for mercy. They stepped back into a single line, like a professional firing squad, and pulled back the trigger on their gun.

Destiny was horrified by what she saw and let out a bloodcurdling scream, "Nooooooo!"

Then she started running towards Jeremy fast as she could. Charles shouted after her, "Destiny!"

When she didn't acknowledge him, he immediately chased after her.

Melissa cried out concernedly, "Charles, what's going on? Charles!"

Charles raised his voice to make sure he was heard. "Melissa, stay there!"

Destiny screamed to the top of her lungs, "Jeremy!"

Suddenly, Charles heard gunfire echoing through the forest. He stopped dead in his tracks. Fear immediately swept through his heart, paralyzing him from going any further.

Destiny could see the bullets hitting Jeremy's body as she continued running towards him. She shouted with all her might, "Jeremy...ask Jesus...ask Jesus...ask Jesus!"

As she got closer to him, the warlocks stopped firing, and Jeremy fell to the ground. Then the warlocks mysteriously disappeared into the dark eerie shadows of the forest.

Destiny dropped to her knees bawling, "No! Lord, please, I don't want him to die without you. You're the only one who can save him from hell."

The young Prophetess sat down on the ground, gently cradling Jeremy's head under her arm while brushing his wavy hair out of his face with her fingertips.

Jeremy slowly opened his pain-filled eyes and looked up at the full moon. Breathing heavily, he managed to force a weak smile at Destiny. With blood spewing out of his mouth, he spoke in a frail raspy voice. "Don't worry, Seer. This time, I didn't bury the knowledge of Jesus Christ. I asked. Tell Charles...."

He hesitated for a moment to cough up some blood and then added, "Thank you, for sharing his treasure with me."

Destiny wiped the tears from her eyes and nodded.

In the next moment, Jeremy gradually closed his eyes and breathed his last breath. As his body went limp, his left arm flopped on the ground, and the black diamond ring fell off his left finger.

When Charles came running up and saw Jeremy dead, he dropped to his knees and started sobbing heavily. "Oh, God, no, please! Now I won't ever see him again."

Destiny hugged Charles and said happily, "Charles, Jeremy didn't die without Jesus."

"Charles wiped his tears and sniffled, "He didn't?"

"No. He asked Jesus into his heart. Jeremy's with us now. He wanted me to tell you, 'Thank you, for sharing your treasure with him.'"

Charles was so overjoyed, he cried out emphatically, "Thank you, Jesus, for saving him."

He gazed up at the stars with a huge grin on his face and then said a quick eulogy to Jeremy. "See you on the other side...buddy."

31

Charles stood in front of the church altar dressed in a white tuxedo, looking very debonair. He had a blood red rose in his hand and could hardly wait for Destiny to arrive. Standing next to him was his best man and two other gentlemen wearing white tuxedos. Melissa was also in the wedding party, accompanied by two bridesmaids. The girls were clothed in beautiful red satin gowns.

Soon as Pastor Sumner stepped upon the altar with an opened Bible in his hand, the *Wedding March* began to play. Then Charles saw the most gorgeous bride he had ever seen come strolling down the aisle, escorted by Elder Ray. She was dressed in a beautiful white satin gown, covered with lace. The white lace had silver specks that shimmered in the light. Upon her head, she wore a headdress of fine pearls that were attached to a long white sparkling veil.

Following closely behind the bride was her maid of honor, who was making sure the long train on Destiny's gown didn't get caught on anything.

After Destiny finished her bridal walk, she strolled over to Charles and whispered something in his ear. Charles immediately gave her a look of delight and said ecstatically, "You're right, Lord. She was worth the wait."

The groom gave his bride the rose in his hand, and she smiled at him while smelling its fragrance. Then he recited a poem he had written especially for her. "You are my destiny, the one God has chosen for me. Our souls will never part, for I shall love you with all my heart. We shall serve the Lord together, through the good times and the stormy weather. I thank God for giving you and me…an eternal destiny."

Charles put the poem into his jacket pocket and then took his bride by the hands. He stared longingly into her eyes, listening intently to the ceremonial words spoken by the Pastor.

"Take the ring and repeat after me," said the Pastor.

Charles reached into his pocket and took out a silver ring with a huge white diamond.

The Minister went on to say, "With this ring, I thee wed."

Charles smiled lovingly at his beautiful bride and resounded, "With this ring, I thee wed."

The groom carefully slid the ring on the bride's right index finger. Soon as they both finished reciting their marriage vows, the Pastor said, "I now pronounce you man and wife. You may kiss the bride."

Charles eagerly took his beautiful bride into his arms and passionately kissed her. Then he took Destiny by the hand and they both turned to face the audience.

The Minister happily announced, "Ladies and gentlemen, I present to you Mister and Misses Charles Chapman.

The audience cheered and applauded the newly married couple.

Melissa whooped and hollered, "You did it Charles! You didn't give up the faith. You're a legend among the stars of faith, a homerun king."

32

Charles turned the page of the paperback titled, *Sting of the Seer*, and continued reading aloud. "As the bride and groom walked down the aisle, the Minister said, 'What God has joined together let no man separate.'"

He closed the book and laid it down on his desk. "Boy, just imagine having your moral sight so magnified you see things for what they really are."

Highly inspired by what he read, Charles rubbed his hands together full of enthusiasm and queried, "Now, can anybody tell me what is unique about this particular writer?"

Tom raised his hand.

"Yes Tom."

"Charter Road always uses deep metaphors in telling her stories."

"So what was the overall message portrayed?"

"I think the writer was trying to tell us that the only way you can be joined to a beautiful destiny is to say, *"I will,"* to Jesus."

"Very good insight, Tom; now does anybody have any questions?"

Several students raised their hands.

Charles pointed to a girl in the front row and said, "Yes Emily."

"Professor, do you really think we need God to find the right destiny?"

Charles picked up the *Holy Bible* off his desk and said, "Without an authentic map, how could you possibly know where to go?"

Emily replied, "So you're saying that everyone needs a charter to guide them down the right road?"

Charles stared at the *Holy Bible* in his right hand and said, . "That's exactly what I'm saying. Jesus is the only clear road that leads to eternal life. All other roads will ultimately lead to death."

The very next moment, the bell rang and Charles said, "Okay, class is dismissed."

After the last class of the day cleared out, Charles sat down and leaned back in his chair, staring at the picture of the rose on the cover of the paperback. He slowly shut his tired eyes and saw a vision of himself. He was strolling down a transparent road, covered in red-letters that were taken out of the *Holy Bible*, symbolic for the spoken words of Jesus Christ. The road passed through the stars and led to a magnificent circular bright light.

Then he heard an audible voice. "For I know the thoughts that I think towards you, says the Lord, thoughts of peace and not of evil, to give you a future and a hope." (Jeremiah 29:11 NKJV)

THE END

Printed in the United States
43510LVS00003B/1-102